W9-CPY-129

NO NEW LAND

BOOKS BY M.G. VASSANJI

NOVELS

The Gunny Sack (1989)
No New Land (1991)
The Book of Secrets (1994)

SHORT STORIES

Uhuru Street (1992)

NO NEW LAND

A Novel

M.G. Vassanji

M&S

Copyright © 1991 by M.G. Vassanji

Originally published in trade paperback with flaps 1991
This B-format paperback edition printed 1994

All rights reserved. The use of any part of this publication
reproduced, transmitted in any form or by any means,
electronic, mechanical, photocopying, recording, or
otherwise, or stored in a retrieval system, without the
prior written consent of the publisher – or, in case of
photocopying or other reprographic copying, a licence from
Canadian Reprography Collective – is an infringement
of the copyright law.

Canadian Cataloguing in Publication Data

Vassanji, M.G.
No new land

ISBN 0-7710-8716-0 (pbk.)
ISBN 0-7710-8720-9 (B-format)

I. Title.

PS8593.A87N6 1991   C813'.54   C91-093267-0
PR9199.3.V37N6 1991

This is a work of fiction. The community described, and
the characters in it, are fictitious, as are the events of the
story. Any resemblance to persons living or dead is purely
coincidental.

The publishers acknowledge the support of the Ontario
Arts Council for their publishing program.

Printed and bound in Canada by Webcom Limited

McClelland & Stewart Inc.
The Canadian Publishers
481 University Avenue
Toronto, Ontario
M5G 2E9

1 2 3 4 5   98 97 96 95 94

For Anil –
who doesn't remember –
and in memory of Auntie

You tell yourself I'll be gone
To some other land, some other sea,
To a city lovelier far than this. . . .

There's no new land, my friend, no
New sea; for the city will follow you,
In the same streets you'll wander endlessly. . . .

– "The City" by C.P. Cavafy, translated by
Lawrence Durrell in *Justine*

What are houses like in Amarapur?

Walls of gold, pillars of silver
and floors that smell of musk.

– Old Gujarati hymn

Acknowledgements

I owe no small debt of gratitude to the International Writing Program at the University of Iowa for its genii-like generosity. I thank Francis, Ahmed, Esmail, Christine, and Simon for inspiration, encouragement, sharing a world.

The Ontario Arts Council, the Canada Council, and the Secretary of State for Multiculturalism have been generous throughout stages of this book.

To Nurjehan, constant companion and patient critic, my appreciation, which is so little a return. Finally, thanks to my editor, Ellen Seligman, for her thoroughness and understanding.

The (Kierkegaard) quotation on page 77 is from *Kierkegaard's Thoughts*, by Gregor Malantschuk, edited and translated by Howard V. Hong and Edna H. Hong, Princeton, 1971.

NO NEW LAND

1

Rosecliffe Park Drive runs its entire short length in a curve, along the edge of a rather scenic portion of the Don Valley. It looks over dense woods which give the valley its many moods and colours; in the distance, from among the trees, rises a lone enigmatic smoke-stack, its activity sporadic and always surprising; a solitary road drops partway down the valley, turns sharply, abruptly ends. A golf course, which appears mostly deserted on the opposite side, lends its simple geometry to the landscape. And down at the bottom, the Don Valley Parkway winds its way hurriedly to the city, which from this vantage point is represented by the single needle-jab into the sky of the CN Tower. On the side facing the valley the drive itself is lined by apartment buildings identified only by their numbers – the famed "Sixty-five," "Sixty-seven," "Sixty-nine," and "Seventy-one" of Rosecliffe Park – whose renown, because of their inhabitants' connections, reaches well beyond this suburban community, fuelling dreams of emigration in friends and relatives abroad. These buildings, when new and modern the pride of Rosecliffe Park – itself once a symbol of a burgeoning Toronto – now look faded and grey, turning away sullenly from the picturesque scenery behind them to the drab reality in front. Barely maintained, they exist in a state just this side of dissolution.

One result of this neglect is that the residents of Sixty-nine Rosecliffe Park Drive are in constant and futile battle against their three elevators. In the late afternoon the confrontation peaks, as residents returning from daily chores pack the lobby and eye with distrust the metal doors in a face-off between man and machine which the latter always wins.

To the people crowding the lobby, waiting anxiously for this reckless and unreliable transportation, it sometimes seems that, against the laws of nature, these elevators go up more times than they go down. Every arriving individual, despairing at the size of the growing crowd, feels compelled to have at least one go at the buttons, both the "up" and the "down." And when one of these donkeys, as these machines are also called, arrives, the doors slide open in a sudden motion that is almost a shouted jeer, and the passengers rush in without priority of age, gender, or time of wait, squeezing in regardless of the weight limit.

In the home of the Lalanis in Sixty-nine, two catastrophes struck on the same day, one more serious than the other. Fatima Lalani was standing squeezed into an elevator on her way up to receive the tidings which she did not as yet know were bad. Her mother Zera had phoned her at the drugstore, where she worked after school, to tell her "it" had arrived, meaning the long-awaited letter from the university, and Fatima took off. In the elevator, although she greeted two small boys and threw a brief but disdainful glare at some of the more ordinary-looking people returning from work bearing parcels of groceries, she was as nervous as she had ever been in her life. It seemed to her that when she opened the envelope which was waiting for her, her entire life would be decided. It did not occur to her that the decision she awaited had already been made a few days before, and she whispered a prayer in much the same way her mother sometimes did; although she had never believed in, in fact had begun to scoff at, the efficacy of this remedy, and her mother was the last role model she had in mind.

Fatima was a tall wiry girl of seventeen. Only the plump ruddy cheeks that stubbornly survived even a near-starvation diet gave evidence of the once chubbiest, and considered healthiest, baby in Dar, the town in East Africa where she was born. It is part

3

of the recent folklore at Sixty-nine that in Canada even the children of pygmies grow up to be six-footers. And good-looking, too. As if to bear this out, Fatima towered over her parents, and in the elevator only one man was as tall as she. She was dressed in designer blue jeans and a stylishly oversized khaki shirt, and her hair was tied in two little clumps by means of bright red clips, enhancing the babyish cheeks.

When the elevator stopped on her floor, two people had to get out to make way, and a pregnant woman with a baby carriage had to squeeze inside further before Fatima could push herself out. Then, with a swing of her shoulders and a shake of her head, as if to banish the odours of cheap perfume and sweat and groceries, she strode off to her apartment. When she let herself in, her mother was waiting like an attendant, envelope in hand. Fatima grabbed it, tore it open, quickly read the gist, and slumped down on the sofa with a loud groan.

"What's it?" asked Zera, her mother, having guessed the answer.

"Arts and Science," spoke Fatima in a mixture of grief and anger tinged with drama.

"So? This is the end of the world then? Arts and Science – what's wrong with it?"

Fatima sulked, picking up the telephone and cradling it in her lap. During the last year, whenever any well-wisher asked her what she wanted to "become," she had given one unequivocal reply: "Become rich." To many of the girls and boys of Sixty-nine and

Sixty-seven and the other high-rise apartment buildings in this part of Don Mills, this is what growing
up meant – making it. To the brighter ones, those
with averages in the eighties and nineties, making it
meant going to university: not to study pure science
or humanities, but something more tangible, with
"scope," computer science or pharmacy for instance.
For the girls, the latter of the two was preferable. It
was more feminine, less threatening to the boys.
Among the brighter girls of Don Mills the competition for a place to study pharmacy at the university is
intense. Fatima Lalani, with an average of eighty-six,
had struck out.

To Zera Lalani, of the old school, any education
was a way out, a way up, and her daughter's disappointment carried no significance beyond her having
to put up with a bout of adolescent sulkiness. Zera
was in her forties and rather plain, with a round
face, long hair tied behind with a black ribbon, a
short body with signs of recently put-on weight. As
she watched her daughter, both feet up on the sofa,
making cautious inquiries over the phone about the
fates of her several friends and numerous acquaintances, Zera had another reason to be depressed. A
little before Fatima arrived the phone had rung.
Someone with a familiar voice she couldn't place at
the time told her that Nurdin would be late.

She had been feeling a little uneasy the past few
days. A premonition. She sometimes got them, she
believed in them. It was about Nurdin. Recently he
had started arriving late from work, bringing with

him grocery items, proof of the shopping that had delayed him. But it was simply not like him to take such an initiative, go off shopping on his own. She felt he was changing. She did not like change. And this evening when she opened the apartment door, she had been hit with an oppressive feeling, a heaviness in the chest, breathlessness without exertion. The premonition. Then the phone call. Better if it had not come. If it was cheap vegetables at Kensington Market that had delayed her husband, the phone call would not have been necessary. Something had happened.

"Leave the telephone now," she said to Fatima, who, startled by the edge in the voice, instantly obeyed.

The door opened, Hanif came in. At fourteen he was as tall as his sister, but bigger: broad and muscular. He went straight to the dining table, saw it to be clear, and turned to his mother: "Oh, you ate."

"No, we are waiting for Daddy. Where were you?" Over him Zera made the greater claim. Their daughter they had perhaps lost already, but she would never lose Hanif. No, not him.

"Oh, at Eeyore's. . . . " He opened the fridge for a snack. Having extracted what he needed, he sat down at the table, surrounded by food.

"Pig," said his sister.

"Pig yourself. I thought we were not speaking."

"Why can't you wait for the rest of us?"

"Because I'm hungry. Where's the old man gone?"

"Ask Mum."

"Hey, Mum, where's Dad?"

His mother turned to look at him. "He's going to be late."

The boy ate and watched her restlessness. Sitting, getting up to do something, forgetting what it was . . . lips pursed, hands clasped in front of her, head raised in a momentary faraway look, in hastily snatched prayer, the large – immense – bosom heaving. He cleared the table and left the room, having thrown a glance at the letter in Fatima's hand. She followed.

"Hey, aren't you going to ask me what it says?"

"No. You can tell me if you want to. Besides, I know what it says."

Then he arrived, much later than usual. He shuffled in, dragging his feet, after fumbling with the lock. Dejection and defeat written all over his face, confirming Zera's dread. He looked like a shrunken version of himself, red eyed and weary, his clothes crumpled, the day's growth of beard bristly on his face. Immediately he was attacked by a barrage of questions and semi-accusations. "Where have you been? What happened? . . . Do you know? . . . We were all . . . "

"Oh, nothing," Nurdin answered hoarsely. He went straight for his armchair and sat down, staring in front of him through the window at the darkness outside, ignoring all further attention. Zera went about setting the table with a little more clatter than usual, and then came and stood in his view, expectantly. He had gathered himself and turned to face her with a pleading look.

"They say I attacked a girl."

"Who?"

"The police . . . and – oh – everyone at work . . . except Romesh."

She realized then it was Romesh who had called her. The kids stood at the doorway now, looking in. They were all quiet for some moments. Finally Hanif broke in.

"She must have done something. Was she rude, Dad? Did she insult you?"

"Your father is not one to attack girls."

"Did you?" the boy asked him.

"Did you?" echoed his wife.

"What kind of question is that?" Nurdin asked irritably.

"Well, what girl?" Fatima exploded. "Where? What happened? Tell us!"

"Later," said Nurdin wearily, refusing to be baited.

Another momentary quiet followed. "What now?" "What now?" The girl and boy asked.

"We must call Jamal," said Zera.

It was some time late that night before husband and wife, alone, found their friend – their former friend, they had to remind themselves, now that he'd moved up in the world – the lawyer Jamal at home, in an irate mood at being called this late. He promised to come the next day.

There was in Nurdin, Zera observed – even after she had heard him relate the incident at work and had heard him answer the children's probing questions – a certain reserve, a disturbing uneasiness, as if he was not telling all, as if he was skirting a certain area, a part of his experience, some part of his life. What was he hiding? Was he guilty? She had never believed she knew all his thoughts, but if called upon she would have guessed his mind, and guessed close enough to satisfy herself. This time was different. He was beyond her and she felt left out. They sat for a long time in silence, side by side, immersed in their own thoughts.

We are but creatures of our origins, and however stalwartly we march forward, paving new roads, seeking new worlds, the ghosts from our pasts stand not far behind and are not easily shaken off. An account of Nurdin Lalani's predicaments must therefore go back in time and begin at a different place.

2

On a stone bench in Dar, at Oyster Bay overlooking the Indian Ocean, two men would quietly sit every afternoon enjoying the cool breeze and each other's company. They were in high spirits and chatty enough when they arrived, but the vastness of the ocean and the rhythm of the wind and the waves and the rustle of the leaves overhead soon drew them in separately, lulling them to stillness, until each man sat motionless, contemplating the expanse in front of them and what lay across it: the land of their birth which they had left a long time ago, to which even the longing to return had been muted, although memories still persisted.

One afternoon the older of the two men breathed deeply from his thoughts, sat back as if exhausted, and then fell sideways towards his companion. The companion let out a startled "Ha!" and then with quick recognition set the old man's head to rest on the bench and quickly took off towards the road to seek help. He was tall, almost bald, and portly in a light blue suit, with a bearing that used to earn the description of "gentleman" in those parts. He was a preacher who had tried his hand at conversion, and was simply called "Missionary" by those who knew him. With a crumpled handkerchief he extracted from his breast pocket he proceeded to flag down the first car that came by. It was driven by a European man and ignored him. Similarly the second. When the third car showed not the slightest indication of slowing down, Missionary simply stepped onto the road. The car braked, and an awkwardly built, gangly European, red faced and in crumpled white trousers and shirt, got out in irritation. It was Mr. Fletcher, the English teacher at the Boys' School, whom he instantly recognized since both his boys went there. Missionary, wiping his face with the handkerchief before putting it away, explained to the teacher what had happened and hastened with him to the bench. They lifted and carried the dead man, Haji Lalani, and lay him on the back seat of the car before proceeding to the nearest hospital, until recently called "European Hospital."

Haji Lalani left behind him three sons, four daughters, and an ailing business. At the time of his death his eldest son was in the Congo, where his fortunes had risen and fallen in recent years with the political fortunes of that newly independent country, and were on the rise again. Nurdin, the middle son, had just given up a hopeless salesmanship up-country. The youngest son was a mechanic, a not entirely honourable profession. The old man, approaching death, had not counted himself very accomplished materially.

Haji Lalani went to Tanganyika as a young man of sixteen in 1906 at the time when the German government there was recruiting Britain's Indian subjects to help build the German empire in Africa. Young Haji apprenticed at an eminent Indian firm in the old slave capital of Bagamoyo. The name Bagamoyo meant "pour your hearts," but no one could say what that referred to – the slaves' grief at having arrived at the market to be sold away to foreigners or simply their relief at having reached the end of the long march. On the east coast of Africa, Bagamoyo was rivalled in eminence only by Mombasa, which was now part of the British colony to the north. In the last fifty years bustling Bagamoyo had received and dispatched slaves in the thousands; it had opened its arms to sultans, slave traders, ivory merchants, missionaries, explorers, and shopkeeper-moneylenders. All roads to the interior departed from here. When Stanley went looking for Livingstone, he left from here; when Burton and Speke went searching for the source of the Nile, they too were waved off at Bagamoyo. But the Germans decided to let the old oriental capital go its way and to build a new European city, at a neglected village with the beautiful name of Dar es Salaam, which would come to be known as Dar. In a parallel move to the north, the British delivered the same fate to Mombasa and developed a railway depot into a European capital city, Nairobi. But Bagamoyo had not given up heart, not as yet. Its citizens, its elders, the imams and the merchants, watched and waited.

Haji went on to become manager of the firm and finally to acquire a shop of his own. He became a man of strict disposition, to whom the harsh German justice – epitomized in the whip made of hippo hide and the name "Hand of Blood" given its wielder by the natives – was not alien in spirit. He could easily have bought a black woman, or acquired one, as some of his compatriots did to while away the lonely nights. He could have taken into his protection a discarded slave woman without a home and fathered a half-breed or two to join the small band that already made up some of the town's youth. Instead he prayed and fasted and became friendly with the fathers at the German Catholic Mission. Any time he could spare from his shop, he spent in theological discussions and friendly debate with the fathers at the mission or with the sheikhs at the mosques.

He himself came from an Indian Muslim sect, the Shamsis, somewhat unorthodox, hence insecure.

Aware that in his good-natured adversaries he had representatives of great and ancient institutions, he would hold his own by maintaining that the truth was known to the few and not the many; its seekers were individuals and not institutions.

One day a young fräulein stopping over at the mission came into the shop to look for gifts for her servants in the European settlement of Wilhelmstal up north, whence she came. She carried a parasol and had the most delicate features. As she stepped in from the glare of sunlight outside, it took a while for her presence to materialize in the relative darkness inside the shop, where Haji Lalani sat with his servant. The girl was accompanied by one of the fathers, who stopped at the doorway to chat, and a servant girl, who carried her shopping. As the fräulein raised her arm to point to a string of beads hanging from a nail, Haji found himself staring at her – she was flushed with the heat, her face lightly perspiring, and her armpit a delicate wet patch – and he felt the faint stirrings of a desire inside him. They did not go very far, in fact he would have quashed these forbidden shadows of thoughts there and then had not his face been brought alive by a stinging slap from the girl's hand. "I am sorry, Fräulein," murmured Haji, eyes smarting, cheeks burning, and the German missionary took the girl away.

"I should have been whipped," Haji later told the church father, who listened in silence. Even saints have been guilty of desire, mused the padre, but of course the crime was not as simple as that.

Many years later Haji told the story to his friend, Missionary, who also listened in silence, perhaps with the same thought as his German counterpart.

Haji Lalani took the advice of the sheikhs of the mosques: to get married and have children is more than half God's religion. He asked the elders of his community to find him a bride. They told him to go to Dar, where he went and approved the daughter of a respectable shopkeeper of modest means. Their first child, a daughter, was born in Bagamoyo. With the German fathers he could no longer consider himself at par, he who had made a virtue of his desire, who was now doubly and would soon be multiply tied to the material world.

War broke out, and the British attacked the German colony from the north, by land. On the ocean British man-of-wars chased German ships and bombarded the towns on the coast. The war on land moved southwards, the bombardments by sea increased, and finally Dar was taken. Haji Lalani and family, British subjects, marched to the capital that was now secure.

The shop of Haji Lalani on Market Street in Dar became a landmark among the busy side streets of the Indian quarter: not for its size or location but because everyone had had occasion to find in it something or other no one else carried. It was the only place where one was guaranteed to find the button of choice, or thread or needle or buckle; it also carried

soaps and shampoos, cough mixtures, tonics, vita-
min compounds, tooth powders and pastes, laxatives
and herb leaves – all from India and England. In all
these years it underwent one change in appearance:
in 1934, the old mud-and-limestone building was de-
molished and replaced by a one-storey structure, with
two flats above the store, one of which was rented out.
As the years went by the white paint blackened and
peeled, and nearby two- and three-storey structures,
more solid looking and broader based, went up
around it, but his building remained a landmark and
Haji Lalani one of the prominent citizens, if known
only inside the Indian community.

He was known for his sternness, which brooked
no nonsense. He went early to mosque, a man slight
of build with weathered face, in his white drill suit
and red fez. He sat quietly against the back wall except when required to come forward to recite or announce, which he did simply and without hesitation,
and returned home early. If ever he stayed late, his
response to the foolery that men generally engage in
while awaiting their more leisurely paced women
would be an acid, cutting remark that would put the
head fool out of commission. Very early he was made
a mukhi, presider of the mosque, for a few years, and
Mukhi Haji Lalani he remained to the townfolk
long after the other mukhis were forgotten.

Haji Lalani's renown and the respect in which
he was held allowed him a certain licence over the
community. He would not hesitate to send away a
loud or rude boy with a cuff, or to scold a girl who

had compromised her modesty by even a glance at a man. So, of his sons, he made examples. Of these, the eldest, Akber, was a textbook case, with whom the father set precedents, often with the help of a cane. The youngest boy, Shamshu, could hide behind female skirts, while the middle son, Nurdin, cowered before his father's wrath, afraid to dare, aware beforehand of the repercussions that would follow.

Above the store, in the flat across from the Lalanis, lived a Hindu family, not Brahmins but humble cobblers, dealers in cowhide. Narandas had two daughters and a younger son. With the second daughter, Nurdin and Shamshu often played. The older daughter was tall and dusky, with a prominent jewelled nose-stud, and a mischievously suppressed smile on her puckered lips as she passed the playing children, holding on to her headscarf. She was liked by the children and talked to them all. Sometimes they could cajole her into casting aside modesty and playing with them. She did not talk to Akber, of course, because Akber was an adult. He was sixteen. A big sixteen with hair on his chest, which you could see because he kept his shirt button open, and who smoked, in secret, affecting styles from the latest Hollywood and Indian films. He was in love with her and pretty certain his affection was returned. For one thing, when he gazed hard at her as she stood at a window she did not look away. And when he was bold enough then to sing out loud "Oh your face among your tresses like the full moon in the night" from a film song, no offence was taken. This form of lovemaking and serenading went on for a few months. Then Akber wrote a note – beginning with a ghazal and ending with "Will you marry me?" He sent it with a servant with specific instructions as to whom it should be handed. The servant headed straight for the opposite flat, without a moment's thought, and the first person he saw there was Narandas's wife. "What do you want?" she asked. He handed her the note. The note ended up on Haji Lalani's lap.

The Germans, in their time, had a standard punishment for offences, called simply "Twenty-five," for the number of strokes of a whip. The British later made their standard an even two dozen, though administered only through the courts. Haji Lalani would sometimes, for example, tell his sons of how a famous Pir punished his only son with one hundred strokes which he completed well past the death of the son, who had dared to consume alcohol. With the lover Akber, Haji Lalani took the German option and beat his son senseless using a schoolmaster's cane. Young Shamshu was whisked to the female quarters, and middle-son Nurdin stood glued, tearfully watching from behind a shelf, muttering "Please, please," wishing his father would stop.

Narandas moved away with his family. Akber was married off to a local girl, and a year later moved to Tabora, inland. Later he went to Belgian Congo.

Fifty years after the store first opened in Dar, business seemed to be waning. Substitutes for what it sold were vast in number, and shops were opening up all over town to sell them. Monkey Brand charcoal tooth powder had to compete with Colgate and Pepsodent; Shikakai soap, by which girls with long thick tresses had sworn for decades, yielded to Lux and Palmolive, advertised by the likes of Sophia Loren at the cinema. To top it all, after the British left, import licences became scarce. Haji Lalani, entering his seventies, did not have the energy to diversify or expand his business, a job for a younger man. Of the two sons who still lived with him, Nurdin withered to ineffectualness under his father's eye and Shamshu was simply a loafer. The shop remained open to give the old man something to do, for which the elderly who had come to depend on it over the years were grateful. His one remaining pleasure was to discuss religion, which he did with others of his age and inclination, and with Missionary, a younger man who had come to Africa during the Second World War.

Of his son, Nurdin – who had survived without giving offence and without special protection – Haji Lalani did not think much. If anything at all, he thought him a good-for-nothing, a bumbler, one likely to drop a cup of tea when serving a guest. But in school and among friends Nurdin Lalani was a middling kind of boy. Neither short nor tall, somewhat skinny, he was not one to take risks but was always game for mischief or a laugh, always with spare change or comic books to lend. He was prone to be the butt of jokes of the rowdier boys, the gang leaders, but these, as he grew older, he learned to manipulate, simply by sharing prudently his generous allowance.

After Nurdin finished school, failing his Junior Cambridge Certificate as many boys did, he tried his hand at various jobs, even at running a business, but with no success. At the prospect of working with his father, he sulked and complained to his mother and sisters. His father finally asked Missionary to find him a job. Missionary, a charismatic, fiery speaker whose fame had spread countrywide, after a few inquiries announced a job for Nurdin: sales representative for the Bata Shoe Company, in Central Province. The job required travel by train and car up-country, and Nurdin was finally free of his father's sceptical eye.

Finally it came time for the young man to get married. Here too Missionary was approached. He ran a class for religion teachers, and he proposed for Nurdin nothing less than his star pupil, Zera. Nurdin acquiesced. His father operated like Fate. To oppose him even for the sake of a gesture would have been to unleash a fury and a storm he had no desire to face. If he probed his innermost desires, then the girl of his dreams was smart and fair, with boy-cut hair, who was comfortable in high heels, spoke English nicely, and perhaps even had been abroad. What hope did he have of that? Zera had none of these qualities. But she looked after and spoke up for him.

And Haji Lalani was elated because he had someone he could make religious talk with, at home.

The place where Haji Lalani died, at Oyster Bay, was a peaceful spot under the gently swaying branches and rustling leaves of two neighbouring trees. They had discovered it together once, he and Missionary, and came whenever they could. It was, according to Missionary's calculation and sure knowledge, one of precisely forty such spots on the face of this earth, whose heavenly bliss, especially after a recent rainfall, was incomparable. Angels, he said, danced in the sunbeams that fell on this sacred place.

When Missionary and Mr. Fletcher placed Haji Lalani's body carefully in the back seat of the car, they placed his fez cap beside him. It was forgotten in the car, and Mr. Fletcher one day returned it to one of Missionary's sons in school. Missionary saw his teenagers playing with the fez, each trying it on, and he retrieved it, sending them away with a few slaps. He kept the red fez as a memento of his dead friend.

It was as if with Haji Lalani a whole era died, a way of life disappeared. Some would say it was the onset of the new era that killed him. Certainly the changes that took place only two years later would have been beyond his wildest dreams.

A few years before, British Prime Minister Macmillan, speaking in southern Africa, hailed the winds of change then sweeping over Africa; in effect, by this very speech unleashing the winds that would accomplish the changes in British East Africa, beginning with independence. By the time Missionary and Haji Lalani's two sons buried the old man, the winds of change had turned into a hurricane. It was a sign of the changing times that Haji Lalani was buried at the new cemetery, an inland site chosen by the new, independent government. At the old, venerated cemetery facing the Indian Ocean, the earth had already been turned, spirits and jinns exposed and rendered powerless, the bones of the Asian dead transplanted to the new site. The only redeeming feature of this new spot, it was said, in the wry humour that usually follows a funeral, was the presence close by of the new Drive-in Cinema, to which the unsettled souls could go to watch India's Rajesh Khanna frolic in the grass with a sari-clad beauty, or America's Charles Bronson mow down his enemies with a machine gun.

The idea of empire was relinquished slowly in the Asian communities. Right up until independence, letters would arrive addressed ostensibly to someone in the "British Empire" or "British East Africa." The Asians had spawned at least two knights of the empire in their slums, they had had Princess Elizabeth in their midst, greeted Princess Margaret with a tumultuous welcome. They spoke proudly of Churchill and Mountbatten, fondly of

22

Victoria. What schoolboy or girl had not heard over the radio the reassuring chimes of Big Ben before falling asleep, or the terrified voice of Dickens's Pip, the triumphant voice of Portia, the Queen's birthday message.

Independence came suddenly but not cruelly. The police and army stayed on, the governor spoke kind words and stayed on as governor general for a year, "Godspeed" said the colonial secretary, Prince Philip waved goodbye. Above all, in the first few days, the newspaper was reassuring, educating people in their new role as citizens of a new country on the world stage, a member of that brotherhood the United Nations, a nonaligned country. It all was fun and excitement, like growing up, being allowed to go out at night, standing up with the adults.

But the winds had only now gathered strength; the fury soon began. The governor general duly left after a year and a republic was declared. On the island of Zanzibar, some twenty-five miles from Dar, a coup finally toppled Arab rule in a bloody revenge by the descendants of the slaves. If it could happen in sleepy Zanzibar, it could happen anywhere. As if confirming the worst fears, within a few weeks followed army mutinies in Kenya, Uganda, and Tanganyika, quelled, embarrassingly enough, with the help of British commandos. During the short-lived mutiny in Dar, looking out, frightened, through their windows, Asians witnessed their shops being looted. Zanzibar, in British and American eyes, became the Cuba of Africa. Cubans were, in fact, rumoured to be on the island, as were Russians, East Germans, and Chinese. Africa is ripe for revolution, said Chou En-lai. Now you could see Chinese men on Dar streets and buy Chinese goods, such as imitations of Parker pens, in the stores. Finally, a new dawn was proclaimed, the beginning of a new era of cultural integrity and economic self-reliance: banks were nationalized, English was replaced as the medium of instruction in primary schools, students underwent army training and political indoctrination, and tilled farms.

They, who had looked to London for the time of day, accepted the changes, the initial ones that came with popular, attractive slogans. Their children, third- and fourth-generation Africans, were taking readily to the new identity. What the government said made sense to the youth. Independence did open up new vistas, intellectually. Swatches of history became available, which had so far been hidden from them. They were not enamoured of the British as their elders were. Not after they had heard or read about Nehru and Tito and Nasser, not to mention Ben Bella and Nkrumah. The future was theirs, they were its masters, and the street fruit-vendor, the shopkeeper, the elderly sheikh all looked upon the schoolchild, black or brown, with pride. Youths would march proudly in support of African socialism in Youth League uniform, under a scorching sun. But as the changes became more extreme, as newer and stranger ways were imposed, the idyll of a new Africa began to appear as shaky to those of the younger generation as it had always appeared to the older.

There were two more disruptive swoops the winds had in store for them, after which they could be said to have done their work.

In Uganda, General Idi Amin, who had overthrown an elected government, had a dream. In this dream, Allah told him that the Asians, exploiters who did not want to integrate with the Africans, had to go. It was said, in an attempt to discredit the revelation, that the general had a few weeks before made an unsuccessful overture to an Asian woman. In Amin's "final solution" the Asians, their citizenships stripped, were expelled – to whatever country that would take them, or else to refugee camps; in effect, they became orphans awaiting adoption. Many of them would wind up in Canada and the United States.

Weeks later, in Dar, rental properties, most of them Asian, were nationalized. There were those whose final act of faith in the new country was to put the savings of two generations of toil to develop a mud-and-limestone dwelling into a two-storey brick building. These buildings lined Dar's main streets, each a monument to a family's enterprise, proudly bearing the family name or else that of a favourite child. When they were taken, that was the final straw. Cynicism replaced faith, corruption became a means.

The "Uganda exodus" showed a way out for Dar's Asians. Canada was open and, for the rich, America too. Thus began a run on Canada.

It was the rich, the hardest hit by the takeovers, who started the movement. Not everyone joined initially, but soon a chain reaction set in, drawing more and more people, fuelled by insecurity, fear, competition, greed, love. Everyone felt the pull. On one hand to see your children using hoes and spades and brooms during schooltime and not learning English when English was one constant you could not deviate from: English education, the one pillar of success, tenet of the faith as it were, becoming more and more inaccessible in the country. On the other hand lay the wealth, the stability of Canada and the Western world. Ten years hence, would your children forgive you when they saw their friends return as wealthy tourists waving dollars and speaking snappy English? The way you spoke English determined who you were. Nurdin remembered: the boys and girls who went to England for their education and returned a class apart – in speech, in clothes, in bearing and manner – in everything. His dream girl had been such a person.

He had been a good employee of Bata. He had developed his market in Central Province patiently, town by town, store by store. He would drive out with his African assistant, Charles, to Morogoro, Dodoma, and towns in their vicinity, trunk and back seat crammed with shoe boxes. He rather enjoyed being on the road. Sleeping in the car, or the backyard in a strange bed in the humble home of a Bata agent; eating in a dimly lit restaurant, under a tree, or at a table under the overwhelming generosity of his host and hostess. There would be the occasional breakdown on the road. In the rainy season you could drive into a ditch. Then you waited hours for help to arrive, on the long-deserted road, or spent a nervous night in the jungle, in the thick impenetrable darkness, encased in the car, straining to hear the distant roar or the closer scratch or rustle, keeping eyes well averted from the window lest a glance outside lock into the ferocious eyes of a devil or an animal. It was always good to have someone with you, and in the morning you felt the stronger for the experience.

With Charles he developed a friendship and came to learn of African ways. Charles, he learned, had about the same education as he had, but was some years younger. Charles too had had a tyrannical father, who was now dead. Most of his life he had spent in a village. He had got the job at Bata through influence, as had Nurdin. Charles had a girlfriend, a university student. In this developing familiarity, Nurdin felt, with some satisfaction, a new experience, a breaking of walls. He let the experience develop its own sure course, take its time. Back home he had two children, a boy and a girl, and a wife who respected him, was affectionate. It was always good to return to them. He looked forward to a permanent return and promotion in Dar, but was hesitant about living under his father's grim rule. This was his life, his lot.

But then came the changes in the country: the nationalizations and the Africanizations. Charles was given the coveted promotion and position in

Dar. Peons, it seemed to Nurdin, rose above him merely because of their black skins. The Europeans had always been masters; their higher positions he had taken as a matter of course. But now in the scramble for promotions he saw himself overlooked, neglected, as a matter of policy, and felt bitter. The quality of shoes had gone down, and customers laughed in his face, showing him the shoddy products of the new government company, holding him to a responsibility his seniors did not respect. Life on the road had lost its charms and he missed Charles. In those tumultuous times it seemed Dar was the place to be. He quit and became a free sales agent in Dar, not waiting for the managership Charles had promised him.

Then his father died. His wife, Zera, ran the shop and Nurdin was all about town looking for odd commissions, spending a lot of time at the middle-aged men's haunt, the A-T Shop, whose tea and kebabs were legendary and where the most up-to-date information on any subject was available.

No one could tell when it happened, but it seemed, suddenly, that a switch had flipped, transforming the mind-set, the worldview: from a position in which Dar was your world, its problems your problems, to one in which leaving became an option, and to many an imperative. There was excitement, restlessness in the air. *Canada*, someone must have whispered the word somewhere. What was Canada – a distant place most did not know where, a pink mass on the map beside the green of Greenland. Suddenly everyone was talking of Canada: visas, medicals, interviews, "landeds." In Canada they needed plumbers, so those who did not know one end of a spanner from another, schoolteachers, salesmen, bank clerks, all joined plumbing classes and began talking of wrenches and discussing fixtures they had never seen in their lives. Toronto, Vancouver, Montreal. You got the most recent news outside mosques after prayers, when men await their women, and during morning and afternoon teatimes at the A-T and other tea shops: who had left, the price of the dollar, the most recent black-market-related arrests. They talked of Don Mills as if it were in Upanga. The buildings of Rosecliffe Park were known, it seemed, in intimate detail. The rich had left almost overnight following the great nationalizations. As the uncertain tension-filled months passed, friends would come to say goodbye, others simply disappeared, and you understood or were told that they had got their landeds and were now probably somewhere in Don Mills.

Zera had taught religion in the schools before; some years after her marriage she took over and infused new energy into the old shop, running it with the help of her mother-in-law. After Haji Lalani's death Missionary still came around, although he now sat to chitchat a few stores away, with another old-timer. He would park his car outside and announce himself to Zera, then go on to have his chat.

She would send a plate of snacks after him, then his second cup of tea, the first cup of course the prerogative of the host. Zera, who in all matters, spiritual or material, deferred to her master's advice, had approached Missionary about a possible move to Canada. "No," he said. "Let the rich go and leave us alone." Zera's sister, Roshan, had already gone with her family and was urging her to come. The rush was on. If you asked the remaining community leaders what to do, they told you somewhat cryptically: "If you're thinking of going tomorrow, go today." Finally Missionary relented. "Soon only the crooks will be left here," he said. "Go."

Haji Lalani, who in his last days would sit at the ocean looking towards the land of his birth with only a twinge of nostalgia ("After all, we've brought India with us"), died believing he had found a new country for his descendants. Two years later, his middle son, with his own family, set off for yet another continent.

3

It was the first flight in an aeroplane, for all of them: Nurdin, Zera, and the two children. Fatima and Hanif, ten and seven, the girl already rid of her baby fat, tall and thin, energetic and demanding, already at this age contentious. The boy affectionate, with a boy's mischief.

"Good night Dar, good morning London": that was the catch phrase they had heard over and over again in cinema advertisements. Comet 4, VC-10, jumbo jet; they had been kept up to date with the advances in jet travel. Now they were inside one of them, on the night plane with its magical lights and reassuring hum, travelling through a darkness as palpable as any he had known in the jungle. Looking out, this time he saw only himself – his reflection.

The Asians, for some reason, had been seated together and for their meal were all fed vegetarian. "Perhaps the meat is pork," murmured Zera. But how, in an airline of a Muslim country? They thought they were taking a friendly airline, Air Egypt, its hostesses bearing names like Farrah and Jahan. But these dyed-blonde, tight-skirted, small-bottomed Farrahs disdained to look at them, and agreed to serve coffee only when the polite and timid raising of hands gave way to a few loud requests accompanied by a ripple of assenting murmurs, so that a protest was seen to be brewing. And then, the embarrassments: to be told like a child how to fasten seat belts and open trays and turn the reading lights on; searching for the toilets, trailing European passengers with your eyes, desperately, waiting until the last moment – like children – before finally plucking up courage, going there and fumbling with the bolts, the hostess lingering to look on and not helping, perhaps later to giggle with her companions; and when inside, not knowing what to do. And later the complaint from the Europeans: the toilets are dirty. Goodness, was Canada going to be like this: every step a mystery and trap, fraught with belittling embarrassments, and people waiting to show you up.

They had to change planes at a terminal in the desert somewhere, outside Cairo, chaotic and crowded as the Dar market, where only American dollars and British pounds were accepted and the change returned in soiled Egyptian notes.

Then finally, with two exhausted children, the flight to London.

They thought they should see London, at least this one time in their lives. London was not a foreign place, not really, it was a city they all knew in their hearts. To hear Big Ben chime for real, see the Houses of Parliament and London Bridge, Buckingham Palace, perhaps the Queen and Prince Philip, and Westminster Abbey where David Livingstone lies buried. London – the pussycat and Dick Whittington, nursery rhymes clamoured in their brains. Zera recited, Fatima corrected. From above, in the plane, as they left the desert of Egypt and Africa behind and flew over the flat, grey and brown wintry fields, neat roads, the orderly rows and squares of staid brick or stone houses, the spires, Nurdin felt a certain foreboding, felt vaguely that he was making a crossing, that there would be no return. Face glued to the window, he watched the world below come alive to the morning's first light: this is Europe. He should make the best of it.

At London airport normal eyes would have seen, at the end of a long queue, a somewhat dowdy couple with puffed faces and two children practically asleep on their feet. What the immigration officials saw, apparently, was a pack of skilled and rehearsed actors from the former colonies out to steal jobs from hard-working English men and women.

First a joint interview – "Why have you come?" "Do you know anyone here?" "Do you have a permanent address in East Africa?" Then interviews, with Nurdin and Zera, in separate rooms, the kids on a bench outside. After that, the frightened kids taken to an inner office for a separate interview. Finally, "I am sorry, sir, you are refused permission to land in the United Kingdom." Words that did not make sense, that cut deeply, for their sheer obstinate wrongness, their boot-like sensitivity. A rubber stamp on their passports to deter future attempted visits. "This way, sir, madam . . . " and onto a departing Air Canada plane.

"The bastards," Nurdin sobbed. "The bastards, the polite British, even when running a noose round your neck, you know how they addressed you back home: 'Your obedient servant, sir, your obedient servant, sir, YOUR OBEDIENT SERVANT!' "

"Nurdin, take a hold of yourself!" hissed his wife.

"The bastards!"

On board the first available plane to Canada he did not even glance outside as they took off. Fifteen years ago he could have come to London as a student and been accepted. What was different now?

In Montreal, the immigration official smiled genially at them. "Welcome to Canada!"

Finally, someone welcoming you, a white man welcoming you. Finally a place to lay down your head.

In Toronto, where they flew straight from Montreal, they were met by a tired-looking Roshan and her husband Abdul. The first thing Zera's sister did when the preliminaries were over was to pass around a pack of chewing gum. "This is Canada," she said, as if mouthing a credo, which indeed it was for her, as they would soon realize.

Snow had fallen, a blistering wind blew squalls on the road and, as they stepped outside the airport building, it made sails of their ill-fitting secondhand clothes, which had seen better days on the backs of colonial bwanas and memsahibs on chilly African evenings. "So this is snow," Zera remarked. It had been cleared into unimpressive mounds and at their feet was a fine powder blown about by reckless gusts. Toes freezing, faces partly paralyzed, eyes tearing, they stood outside, shoulders hunched. The two children were moaning and shivering, weeping, hiding behind adult coats, creating fresh pockets and exposing fresher areas of anatomy for the wind to snatch at. After the projected taxi fare was mentally converted to shillings, they opted for a bus. And finally the embracing warmth of a heated bus, heating every pore, releasing by delicious mechanisms every shiver out from it. In a semi-dazed state, Nurdin watched the yellow streetlights and the snow-flakes and the myriad of cars on highways winding around each other like ribbons, like nooses, if you please, your obedient servant. Big Ben says eighteen hours Greenwich mean time, and Father looks up, raises an eyebrow, if you please, and shush, everyone listens to perfect inflections from the BBC, you dare not scrape or cough at this holiest of hours at home and you hold your water and your bowels and your wind, and if a giggle escapes, then the wrath of God, Haji Lalani's cane on your buttocks until you cry out Mercy, mercy, Father, but Haji Lalani will complete his quarter-century – Mercy, wails the lover Akber, but the strokes keep coming, regulated, calculated, for it is God's punishment and Akber lies comatose, Father falls back exhausted, and you become aware of the wetness between your thighs.

"Aré, Hanif, you could have waited," Nurdin said to his son, but the boy slept peacefully on his lap.

The next morning, in Roshan and Abdul's Don Mills apartment, the sun shining brightly, deceptively, through the balcony's sliding doors, an abundant breakfast on the table – with toast and eggs and juice and jam and parathas – Zera practically danced through the two kitchen doorways, going out this one and in the other, saying wow, this is big, gorgeous, a refrigerator, a television, new sofas, dinette.

"But you have everything," she said to her sister, still dancing in the doorways.

"Aré, you should see how the others live . . . carpet wall-to-wall, not an inch uncovered." She emphasized, eyes flashing: "Not one bare inch, and console television and – "

"Wah," said Nurdin, lounging on the sofa. "This is enough for me. This is all I ask for."

"Wait," said his sister-in-law, "you'll want more. And you'll get it. This is Canada."

Nurdin eyed the two women. They had such affection for each other, spoke so freely to each other. No one could have guessed they were sisters. Zera, round face and soft body, had that twinkle in her eye and dimples and the puckered half-shy smile that won everyone over. It certainly brought forth his affection for her. Roshan, taller and stronger, was some years older. She had been their father's child by a previous mother, rarely mentioned, but a black woman, as everyone guessed. Perhaps a kept woman. Roshan had a dark complexion, which she tried unsuccessfully to lighten, using loads of makeup and creams, and wavy hair she tried desperately to straighten and lighten. She had large front teeth that simply wrecked her smile, and a dark scar on one cheek where Zera had burned her with a spatula in a girlish squabble long ago. Perhaps to deflect attention from her face, she wore loud and garish dresses.

Roshan's husband, Abdul, was a mechanic and had a job as mechanic's assistant and gas pump attendant. In Dar, he had been head mechanic at Datsun. A dour, private man, tall and balding, depressive. He had been married before, a marriage that lasted a few days, for reasons that could only be guessed at. He carried a secret, deep hurt that no one could ever fathom. Roshan worked at a factory. They had two children, a boy and a girl.

Within a week, Fatima and Hanif were admitted to school, Zera found a job as a receptionist, and proper winter clothes were bought. They thought they would stay with the in-laws until Nurdin found a job, or the financial crunch relaxed, but it was not easy. The four children fought over practically everything, but mostly the television. And Abdul was a difficult man. Finally things came to a head, and they had to leave.

One Friday evening Roshan had been ironing the pants for her husband to wear to the mosque, when a loud cry and a fight broke out among the children before the blaring television set. All four were on the sofa, in a screaming sobbing tangle of arms and legs. The two women ran to the rescue and in the meantime the iron tipped and burned a pant leg. Abdul went over, picked up the pants, and held them in the air.

"What is this?" he said, coming slowly towards Roshan, a sneer of contempt on his face.

"Oh, the children were – "

He landed a tremendous smack on her face. You could see it smarting, swelling with the hurt, tears in her eyes.

There was absolute silence, the children were terrified. Roshan stood nursing her cheek, Nurdin turned to look at his wife and saw Zera in a rage, lunging at Abdul with the hot iron. Nurdin moved to block her way, barely missing getting burned himself, and Abdul was saved. A loud quarrel ensued, threats and abuses were exchanged, and the police were almost called. Roshan cried and Zera cried and the children wailed.

In such quarrels, where he was obviously at fault, Abdul had a simple stratagem. He would go out and sulk in the corridor. In Dar, he would go for a drive, leaving Roshan extremely worried, since it was usually at nighttime. "Leave him alone," said Zera. "Let him be," said Nurdin. But for how long? Finally, to save embarrassment, Roshan went out to her husband, and the two talked in whispers for close to half an hour, huddled like young lovers, before Abdul agreed to come back inside. It turned out that he had a grievance against the Lalanis for not contributing to household expenses, and letting Fatima bully his children.

"But you refused to take money," Nurdin protested. "And we do buy groceries. We were saving to buy you a present even though I am not yet working."

The next day they had to search for an apartment and move. They came to Sixty-nine Rosecliffe Park Drive, a building some fifteen minutes' walk away. The money they had brought with them from Dar and hardly touched now went to pay the deposit and the first month's rent.

4

What would immigrants in Toronto do without Honest Ed's, the block-wide carnival that's also a store, the brilliant kaaba to which people flock even from the suburbs. A centre of attraction whose energy never ebbs, simply transmutes, at night its thousands of dazzling lights splash the sidewalk in flashes of yellow and green and red, and the air sizzles with catchy fluorescent messages circled by running lights. The dazzle and sparkle that's seen as far away as Asia and Africa in the bosoms of bourgeois homes where they dream of foreign goods and emigration. The Lalanis and other Dar immigrants would go there on Saturdays, entire families getting off at the Bathurst station to join the droves crossing Bloor Street West on their way to that shopping paradise.

The festival already begins on the sidewalk outside: vendors of candy, nuts, and popcorn; shop windows bright and packed; shoppers emerging, hugging new possessions; and bright signs with all the familiarity of hookers clamouring for attention. "Come in, don't just stand there!" shouts a sign wickedly. "Come in and get lost!" winks another. And in you go, dissolve into the human tide flooding the aisles and annexes. You enter a crowded bright tunnel of a passageway lined with record jackets and throbbing to a loud, fast rhythm, the tide draws you in, the music lulls your mind, sets you in the mood, deeper and deeper you go into the tunnel, which opens onto a large cavern busy with the frenzy of buying. After a lifetime of waiting, it is easy to get drawn in blindly, forgetting what you came for, lured from every side by cheeky price labels and imagining new needs for the home. Buying is a narcotic, so you have to be quick and know your business, pick out the genuine sales from the spurious, think of your budget and your needs. Many times you'll catch yourself in temptation: A bargain, but do I need it? No, you steel yourself, you put it back. Several times at this and you're one of the pros, walking easily up and down the aisles, into and out of the annexes, from the basement to the top floor and back . . . in this place so joyous and crazy where people give free unasked advice, and just as freely demand it.

The first few times they would stand in wonder before the racks, piles, and overflowing boxes and crates, fingering perfectly good clothes for sale for peanuts, as it were: shirts for $1.99, dresses for $4.99, men's suits for $14.99! Compare with the headaches you could buy in Dar with such difficulty: size sixteen shirts with size fourteen sleeves, pockets sewn shut, flies too short, shoes not matching, zips not closing. Even after converting dollars into shillings, at black-market rates, you couldn't beat these prices. Cheap, cheap, cheap, as the sign said. No more haggling over prices; you just had to know where to go. And this was it. They began to buy. Business runs in the blood, they are former shopkeepers after all, and the thrill of chasing a bargain is irresistible, a pleasure which sharing can only enhance. News of special bargains, the not-to-be-missed sales, passed by human telegraph from aisle to aisle – Bai, the women's underwear is on special, way over there behind the coats, you won't get such sizes anywhere at any cost, so-and-so has dropped one on the floor for you, just in case. Beats sewing your own.

Where else could you stock up your kitchen, buy your winter wardrobe, add the luxury of a few ready-made clothes, while looking for a job?

From Ed's to Knob Hill Farms for groceries, by subway and bus, clutching coupons, purses, bags, and kids, running up and down aisles gritty with spilled grain and discarded peanut shells, hunting down specials, past boys and girls tasting and filling up with as much as they could. For limited quantities whole families appeared, toddler to grandma, emerging each with a can of oil, a bag of sugar, whatever.

And later still, if there was a job in the family, and money flowed a little more easily, a stop at Consumers Distributing: a TV stand, a toaster, an iron.

From their apartment, through the living-room window and the balcony, the Lalanis could see, penetrating through a mass of foliage in the distance, the top of the CN Tower blinking its mysterious signal. In rain or shine, a permanent presence in their lives, a seal on their new existence, the godhead towards which the cars on the parkway spilled over, from which having propitiated they came racing back.

After their initial excitement, the days of wonder when every brick was exotic and every morning as fresh as the day of creation, came the reckoning with a future that they'd held at bay but was now creeping closer. They had come with a deep sense that they had to try to determine it, this future, meet it partway and wrest a respectable niche in this new society. First the man of the house had to get work befitting his status. But try as he might, Nurdin Lalani could not find a job. The first few rejected job applications he took in stride: a few disappointments only to enhance the sweetness of eventual success. But the pattern persisted, and slowly in his mind the barest shadow became discernible, of impending despair, the merest possibility of a jobless vista ahead, but nonetheless frightening.

Patience, they tell you, those who've been here before you. The women are always in demand, as typists and clerks, even babysitters, changing jobs with ease, confidently picking up the new ways, never looking back from their new freedom. But look around you. It takes months before the men uncertainly settle down at work they'll never be satisfied with. . . .

You check the mail hopelessly, before taking your bus to meet the jobs head-on. These are the first days and you hate yourself for arriving in winter. Braving the punishing cold, you beat the footpaths, searching for vacancies. You do Yonge Street, then Bloor, Dundas, and Queen, the East End, then the West. Taking refuge in donut shops, using precious change to make phone calls doomed by the first word, the accent. I am a salesman, I *was* a salesman. Just give me a chance. Why don't they understand we can do the job. "Canadian experience" is the trump they always call, against which you have no answer. Or rather you have answers, dozens, but whom to tell except fellow immigrants at Sixty-nine. You try different accents, practise idioms, buy shoes to raise your height. Deodorize yourself silly. On these hopeless treks, how many times you've sniffed the air outside a restaurant, wishing – oh, shame of shames! – you could afford a hamburger, a hot dog, french fries. But the price of a hamburger here could buy four at Dominion. Sweaty, dishevelled, tired, and desperate – a state you had never known in Dar – you go home and wait for the kids. You clean up, do laundry, do anything, so as not to appear useless. Then she arrives, the breadwinner, tired, rightfully so, but will she understand your fruitless exhaustion? Over dinner you jealously hear her talk, full of the new life. You look sideways at her: do you see contempt, or merely pity?

Mr. Rogers of Eatons was a tall big-boned man with large feet and hands. Do they all have to be so tall? Nurdin thought to himself. In Dar, the short took refuge in the saying: "Too tall, too stupid." Mr. Rogers was polite: "Gentleman," the word formed itself in Nurdin's mind. Perhaps his candid and easy manner – lack of arrogance, unlike those whites at Sixty-nine – belied a little stupidity?

He was being interviewed at the shoe department of the downtown store, a job simply tailor-made for him, he thought; there was no job he had felt so qualified for. Mr. Rogers had asked him about his experience, had heard all about his Bata salesmanship, and was now escorting him to the seventh floor to fill out some forms. Nurdin was bubbling with excitement and enthusiasm. Mr. Rogers appeared to be a man in his late fifties, elderly, and inspired in Nurdin a feeling of genuine respect. He already saw himself working under this fatherly figure. It was this that made him gregarious that morning. He wanted to show this man that he could talk, was capable.

"The safari shoes," he was saying to Mr. Rogers pointedly, detailing his past experience on their way to the elevators, "seemed to go best of all – "

"Indeed," said Mr. Rogers.

"Because, you see, they don't show the dust – "

"We don't have much of that here," Mr. Rogers said in good humour.

If only he would let me finish. "Yes, yes, and they became fashionable, you see, because John Wayne wore them in the film *Hatari* – "

"I don't believe I have seen it."

He felt he had to keep talking, get closer to the man, develop this first-time meeting which had started so well, beyond his wildest dreams, into something solid and permanent. He had never talked with a white man on such terms before – sure, the super at Sixty-nine, and some of the cashiers in stores, but not to a real white man, a gentleman – and he was simply carried away.

They took an elevator filled with a clutch of well-dressed elderly ladies.

"Good morning, ladies," Mr. Rogers called out and checked if the button for his floor had been pushed.

"I can tell good leather just from a single look," Nurdin told him unabashedly.

"Indeed."

"Now there," said Nurdin, pointing to the man's well-polished brogues, "that is a good leather."

Mr. Rogers grinned. "I should say so, I paid a good buck for them."

There was no stopping him now.

"You see, when I was young, we had our shoes handmade by a cobbler," Nurdin grinned. "It was wo̶mmy. Every day I or my brothers went to ask ... are the shoes ready?' And every day he

"This wa,̶̶ ̶row.' Finally – "

loud voice to the ei̶uMr. Rogers beckoned with a stopped, standing against the door ̶omen as the elevator with a slight bow in an act of exaggerated courtesy. "Straight ahead and to your right!"

"As I was saying," continued Nurdin, when the women had gone and the elevator was on its way up again, "finally I would get fed up and say, 'Uncle, if they are not ready, don't bother.' "

The elevator stopped and he followed Mr. Rogers out. The man was taking long strides and calling out to people he knew on this floor, making Nurdin acutely aware of his short stature.

But he would have his say, even though he realized by now that Mr. Rogers was not really interested. "And you know what? The cobbler would give a look of protest. 'But these ones, they are yours!' he would say and point to the shoes he was making just then. But, listen, of course they were not mine!"

They had arrived at a tall counter, from where Mr. Rogers picked up an application form for employment. Across from it were a table and chair. When Nurdin had filled in the form he asked Mr. Rogers if he would get the job.

"There are many other applicants, you know. But we'll call you. Keep your fingers crossed!"

"Fingers crossed, eh." Nurdin demonstratons grinned in a final gesture of good hum

When he didn't hear for a wee' and asked for the shoe depar. Rogers said, "we gave

"I'm afraid, Nurdin the job to someone

Nurdin exploded. "But my experience! I know shoes, I can give references – "

"I'm sorry, there were many applicants."

"I know I don't have Canadian experience," he breathed hotly and with emotion on the phone, "but how can I get Canadian experience if you don't give me a chance? I've sold shoes for eight years! Eight years – "

"Perhaps you were overqualified, sir."

That was a new one. Overqualified. Good for laughs, and it got many.

The phone rang one day.

"Hullo," said a cautious voice at the other end. "Am I speaking to Mr. La-la-ni?"

"Yes, this is Mr. Lalani."

"How are you, Mr. Lalani?"

"I am quite well, thank you," he answered, exactly as he had been taught in childhood.

"Good! My name is John McCormack, Mr. Lalani, and I would like to invite you to a party."

"A party. . . ." He thought it might be some church group up to a new trick.

African immigrants appeared in the limelight for a brief period when the Uganda refugees started arriving. In the basements of churches, welcoming committees got busy. Clothes and food were collected, Bibles ordered. What were expected, after subway posters and newspaper ads showing photos of starving and naked pot-bellied children with runny noses, suffering dreadful diseases like beriberi and kwashiorkor, were hungry pagans. What the church groups saw were healthy-looking people, some thin, no doubt, and bow-legged, but many – especially women – were heavy, and some positively chubby. The refugees took shelter and disappeared into the developments of Don Mills, Willowdale, Brampton, and Mississauga, there to be joined by fellow Asian immigrants from Africa.

At Sixty-nine Rosecliffe Park and its neighbours the new immigrants were beset by hosts of proselytizers. They came from several different sects, singly or in packs, using all manner of approaches, bearing literature and tidings, goodwill and goodies, warnings and mercy. But in the Dar immigrants these missionaries met a litigious lot, for they love to debate, and they debate nothing better than community politics and religion. Zera would be in

...matched form. She could tell of her [miss]ionary's legendary public debates in *Master Da...* [against] sheikhs, pandits, priests, and scientists. So when the Bibles were produced, they were grateful[ly accepted]. But somewhere in the ensuing discussion, the conversation took a wrong turn and became – pointless. For one party it showed no direction, no purpose. For the other, it was simply – fun. We also have a God. We have a Pope too. Don't you know that Prophet Muhammad (upon whom be peace) is predicted in your Bible? What you've got, we've got too, only more modern. We change with the times. So the invitations ceased, dry muffins and cakes stopped arriving: the proselytizers gave up in frustration. All, that is, save three hardy ladies, two black and one white, who came Saturday mornings. Get trapped into a religious argument with that threesome on Saturday, and you practically starve the following week for not having bought your groceries. From apartment to apartment telephone lines buzzed with alarm as soon as these harbingers of hell were sighted getting off the bus, waddling towards the buildings, gravely bearing their packages of books and pamphlets full of warnings.

"A party," said the friendly voice of John McCormack, a little more forcefully this time, bringing Nurdin back from his thoughts. "A party where new Canadians can meet the old and learn from their experiences. A party to welcome the newcomers. This country was made by immigrants like you, Mr. Lalani."

He gave directions. "Would you like us to invite anyone else you know, Mr. Lalani? The more the merrier, as we say."

"My wife's sister and her husband, Mr. and Mrs. Abdul Ismail."

"Oh, the Ishmaels. They've already been invited. Anyone else you can think of?"

"No."

"Well, goodbye. And see you on Thursday!"

"See you on Thursday. Thank you Mr. McCormack!"

"John."

". . . ."

"John. Call me John."

"See you Thursday, John! Thank you!"

The party was at the Don Mills Inn on Eglinton Avenue, a short brisk walk away, except there are no sidewalks on Eglinton there and you are exposed to cars whizzing past. They were with Roshan and Abdul. They needed Roshan yet, her boisterous confidence, if not entirely convincing, was at least enough to draw attention away from themselves in unfamiliar situations.

They entered through revolving doors into a large lobby brilliantly illuminated by a central chandelier and numerous wall lights. Dazed by the sudden brightness, they stood back, uncertain, bewildered.

And terribly impressed by what they saw. "Wow!" muttered Roshan, a little too loudly. "This is what I call posht." The carpet under them was a plush red. In the distance was the reception desk, large and busy, impressively modern. People sat and stood, merry pageboys in green and gold sauntered around, the elevators pinged. An attendant came towards them, and instinctively they all drew a little closer together. Nurdin thought nervously of his suit. A bargain, though the checkered design was not to his complete liking. And the sleeves were just noticeably long. If he had come alone or even with Zera only, he would have fled. This was not for him, an atmosphere that made him so conscious of himself, as if he was onstage and those people were the spectators. He had moved a little behind Roshan, who was dressed in a bright olive green bargain and had on her most garish makeup. Also taking refuge behind her was Abdul, while Zera stood a little to one side taking everything in. The man politely but firmly pointed out the escalator: "Up and the last door in the corridor."

Crossing this first obstacle gave their spirits a boost. Standing clumped together, though breathing easier, they looked down on the lobby as they went up the escalator. Tall ladies in furs, men in tweeds and leathers, fawning attendants. It could have been a scene from a movie or from a magazine ad. Yet from afar it looked easier to feel part of it, and they felt a glowing sense of privilege. The time was not far behind them when they could not even have imagined being in such a place, so close to those people. Upstairs, following instructions, they pushed through a heavy padded door into another brilliantly lit room. At the door was a small table where they had to check in.

"Obviously no riffraff here," said Roshan approvingly.

Their names were duly ticked in the guest register, and they were admitted to the party. A tall handsome man in a blue suit and bow tie, somewhere in his forties, started towards them, all smiles and goodwill. It was John McCormack himself. "Welcome, welcome folks. Come and meet your fellow Canadians." He insisted on pronouncing each of their names correctly, at which they were touched.

There were two long tables at right angles covered with red cloth. A hundred or so people must have been present, of all races it seemed, from every corner of the world, milling around, forming tentative groups, talking of the new experience. The thrill of it all, like the first day at school. "So I told her, 'What do you need a fridge for, woman? Just leave the food outside the window, it's cold enough!' " "Imagine a squirrel eating donuts!" "Man, where I come from, only millionaires could afford donuts!" "To London and back, so fast? What did you take – the Concorde? 'Ha! Gray Coach,' I said!"

Suddenly some carts came trundling along, pushed by the gilded attendants, plates were unloaded on a table. Food rolled in next and was unloaded: trays of salad, hors d'oeuvres, cold cuts.

A small circle formed around the table, a group of shy, hesitant guests. But this was the barest beginning, even as they watched, the circle became denser and denser. Roshan soon disappeared and the remaining three of them stood shy and uncertain, not knowing what to do, waiting for the rush to end, gnawed at by hunger and anxious for food. A tall elderly black man, whose height was an obvious asset in such situations, passed by, plate loaded. "Dig in," he grinned. But the crowd there had already dug in, three deep, jostling and cussing, every man and woman for themselves, coming out mauled and with a plate only partly full.

"The Third World, man," said the black man, with a wink. He had found himself a seat nearby, and spoke with a full mouth as he took in the scene, mightily amused. Watching him eat with such relish only accentuated their hunger, and they felt rather irritated and without hope of ever eating that night.

And then from somewhere came Roshan, sailing towards them, grinning with her big teeth, saying through purple-painted lips which hardly moved, so no one else could hear: "The other table, quick, the other table at the end, before they all rush there!" As Nurdin stood staring at those purple lips struggling to decipher their message, his wife urgently pulled him by the sleeve, and soon there was food before them.

"Pile up, pile up!" ordered Roshan. "There won't be another chance." Sure enough, turning around with heaped plates in their hands, they barely escaped the onslaught.

When the tables were cleared and moved away, civility returned to the hall, as before, with subdued, controlled intercourse. The whole dining interlude that preceded now seemed like a crazy dream.

A red carpet was rolled out and a fashion show was announced, its theme "The Complete Canadian Male or Female." The guests voiced hearty approval at the change of pace and gathered around to watch. Winterwear from fur ("the ultimate in elegance") to artificial fur ("affordable elegance, or to have your cake and eat it too"), leather ("warm and cool in the fast lane") and wool ("elegance and reserve") were shown. Underwear ("Let's face it, ladies, we all like to feel *good* inside") from silk ("for the precious you") to cotton ("for the sensible") to blend ("for the practical").

"Shameless bitches," Nurdin heard a voice say through clenched teeth as the models traipsed in on high heels, wearing roguishly girlish smiles on their faces, to show the latest in inner comfort. You cannot look too hard, you cannot look away, he thought uncomfortably to himself. One or two audible jolly masculine approvals are voiced, for which diversion you are thankful. He thought he had heard Zera express the intense disapproval, and perhaps Roshan also said something similar. Then, "After this brief session," a bazaar was announced, where some of the previously exhibited ware was put on sale. Simultaneously a cash bar was opened and a dance began. At this point they decided to leave.

"This is the kind of thing we have to steer our kids from," Zera said, elaborating on her previous remark.

"Precisely, sister," said Roshan. "We have something to give too to this country. Morals, I say." She stabbed a finger at the air, to emphasize.

"The bikini girls are dancing now," Abdul remarked, looking away a little too reluctantly, as Nurdin noted.

"With clothes on?"

"Yes."

"How shameless can they get. With the same men who were ogling at them."

At the door sat the woman who had let them in, cashbox in front of her.

"Ten dollars, please," she said to Roshan, who was leading the way.

"What ten dollars?" replied Roshan scornfully. Her ire had really been roused.

"Madam, you ate food here and were entertained – "

"What food? We had to run for crumbs like chickens – you call that food?"

"I am sorry but – "

"*I* am sorry. And you show a procession of naked women – "

"That was a fashion show, not a procession of naked women."

"In knickers, with our husbands watching, showing thighs up to here." She demonstrated, running a finger over her dress. "That is not naked? You want to show more, you shameless woman?"

At that point Mr. McCormack came genially by.

"I am not a shameless woman and those were not naked women," said the cashier at the top of her voice, taking strength from this intrusion.

"Excuse me ladies – and gentlemen. Is there a misunderstanding?" said Mr. McCormack, drawing them together around him.

"I think there has been, sir," said a firm voice. Its owner joined the scene. "My name is Jamal. How are you, sir." He shook hands with Mr. McCormack.

"Ah, Jamal," said Nurdin. The name was familiar, as was the face. One of the educated younger generation.

Jamal had fiery black eyes and a droopy black moustache. He was big, fair skinned, and dark haired. In an immaculate striped suit and red tie, he looked impressive.

"I am a lawyer. These are all" – he put his arms around as many of them as he could – "my . . . potential . . . clients."

"Jamal," Roshan turned on him, speaking in Gujarati, "are you going to let these thieves chisel us out of ten dollars each?"

Jamal acknowledged the gesture of confidence but kept to English.

"They can't charge you a penny, go home, go home." He went to join the friend he had abandoned in order to come to their rescue.

Mr. McCormack had meanwhile been talking with the woman at the table. He came up once more and raised his arms to draw them closer around him again. "There has been a misunderstanding. There is no charge. The lady was following a prior arrangement which had been changed. . . . "

So that was how they met Jamal. In Dar they had known him, but vaguely by face and mostly by reputation. In Toronto they would come to know him well.

5

Sixty-nine Rosecliffe Park. The name still sounds romantic, exotic, out of a storybook or a film. Sometimes it's hard to believe you are here, at this address,
sitting inside, thinking these thoughts, surrounded
by luxury: the carpeting, the sofas, the telephone, the
fridge, the television – yes, luxuries by Dar standards
– things you could not have owned in a lifetime. The
CN Tower blinks unfailingly in the distance; the
parkway is incredibly beautiful at night: dotted lines
of glowing lights curving in the darkness of the valley. And when it's snowing there in the night, softly,
silently, whitely, you wonder if it's not a childish

Christmas card you are dreaming. But then you step out in the common corridor with its all too real down-to-earth sights, sounds, and smells, and you wonder: *This*, Sixty-nine Rosecliffe? And you realize that you've not yet left Dar far behind.

"Twenty floors." Nurdin once did a small calculation for his wife. "Twelve homes in each – you have two hundred and forty families – that's three good-sized blocks of any street in Dar." Except that the variety found here at Sixty-nine would not be found in any street in Dar. Here a dozen races mingle, conversant in at least as many tongues.

For many of life's amenities, there are enough local enterprises busy all day in this upright village to service all kinds of needs. This means that not everybody leaves the building to earn a living, or buy a service, and during the day life and excitement do not vanish from the corridors of Sixty-nine. From which fact Nurdin, unemployed for many months, could draw some comfort.

On the sixth floor, well along the corridor and away from the bustle of the elevators, runs the major local industry. Here one Gulshan Bai prepares full meals for two, to take out. Back in the days when servants cooked over huge coal and wood fires, more than thirty customers took away tiffin daily from Gulshan Bai's Dar residence. Tiffin was carried in a metal contraption, four cylindrical boxes fitting one on top of the other, the last one with a lid, all run at the sides by two rods which met at the handle. Now the tiffin boxes are simply the plastic ice cream and yoghurt containers. And Gulshan Bai minds the stoves herself, sweaty and red faced, perhaps not as cheerful as she used to be, and the flesh on her arms is a little tougher, but still ripples away as she rolls the chappatis every day.

The times are gone also when chappatis came thin and soft as hankies, and could be folded as such; when every time the last piece of the last chappati disappeared into your mouth, a fresh one from the stoves appeared on your plate. Now on the fourteenth floor, Sheru Mama dispenses chappatis at four for a dollar, cheaper wholesale. Sheru Mama makes hundreds of chappatis every day and babysits two toddlers at the same time, while husband Ramju helps with the dishes and puts the required dollop of margarine over every chappati. Her customers tend to be single men who will eat a chappati with a pickle, or butter and jam, or curry canned in the U.S.

The building has a peculiar incident as part of its lore. It happened before the Lalanis' time. Several men had complained of waking up some mornings with a heart heavy with nostalgic yearnings and a clear memory of a Dar backyard strewn with grains and busy with the frantic clucking of hens. Why the persistence of that memory, so sharp and clear, over many others? This became clear when a local tabloid arrived one morning with the sensational headline: VOODOO IN DON MILLS! Apparently a gang of boys had come upon a site covered with blood and feathers in Rosecliffe Park, behind one of the apartment buildings. And then one realized, or was patiently made to realize by those more experienced in the ways of Rosecliffe, that the mystery of the nostalgic dream had a simple solution: halal meat – meat from a correctly slaughtered animal, neck slit open with a sharp knife, blood allowed to gush out, appropriate verses recited by the slaughterer with his head covered. So the clucking hens were real Ontario hens, and those who could have sworn they'd heard a cluck or two in the elevators were probably right.

You can buy halal meat now, from Ram Deen, an Asian man from the Caribbean. You knock on the door decorated with two suras from the Quran in Arabic calligraphy and one in English in luminous green and gold lettering, and an I LOVE ALLAH sign; a head covered with Muslim modesty pops out with a wooden "Yes?" to which you tell your halal needs. It searches the corridor suspiciously and looks you up and down. It is usually Ram Deen's young daughter, doing a mental calculation to check if you are a "brother." If you are deemed not, she tells you her father is not in. If you are passed, the door closes, and a few minutes later out comes Ram Deen himself, a short thick man with a pointed greying beard, in a clean white smock, with your package neatly wrapped and a smile of appreciation. There is a practice at Sixty-nine to smile behind his back, but with restraint, for the last thing you want to do is to be caught laughing at a butcher, and a holy one at that.

If you are suddenly out of toilet supplies, you can run down to the first floor and buy them at almost all hours from an apartment there. There are places to order snacks or go and eat them. There is an open house on the eighteenth floor every Saturday night, where over a spectacular view of the valley, with its orange-lighted highway, you can play cards, chew the fat with compatriots, or tease the women, and consume tea and samosas, which you have to buy there. There are babysitters on every floor, and housesitters; accounting or legal advice, a nurse, a genuine practitioner of folk medicine who will pray or knead your pains away.

In the mornings outside the elevators, the mothers of Sixty-nine stand hovering round their broods, eyes shining with pride, adding finishing touches to their morning's work, a flourish here, a button there. And they all go down at about the same time. At five to nine a gang of mothers, a few unemployed fathers, and some grandparents accompany the horde of children to the nearby elementary school, yelling, scolding, cuddling. They march to that part of the street where another grandfather does service in an orange jacket, wielding a stop sign, controlling traffic rather proudly as if fulfilling a childhood dream, and the kids cross the road and race through the school gates.

One envies these children, these darlings of their mothers, objects of immigrant sacrifice and labour, who speak better-sounding if not better English: one envies them their memories when they are grown-up. Take this girl in hijab, standing in the elevator, head covered, ankles covered, a beautiful angular face, long body, who could have come straight from northern Pakistan. But when she opens her mouth, out flows impeccable Toronto English, indistinguishable from that of any other kid's, discussing what? – last night's hockey game. In her arms, covered with a decorated green cloth, is a heavy book also apparently in hijab. She's on her way to Quran class, on the fourteenth floor. What will she remember when she is twenty, thirty, what will she write?

Five o'clock at Sixty-nine. In the lobby, traffic is at peak because schoolchildren are still coming in and office workers from the Don Mills area are beginning to join the elevator queues. The three elevators have been taking a beating since three. They bring, every time they open their doors, fresh waves of food smells to assail the nostrils of the waiting crowd.

There are those, usually immigrants, who find the smells simply embarrassing. There are those who have grown old here, who walk helplessly by, chins up, wondering what it was they did to deserve the brunt of such an invasion. Some residents come home to Sixty-nine to the reassuring clutches of the friendly vapours, and then go up and have a good meal. And finally there are the visitors, couples who come to take their toddlers from the friendly, homely curry-smelling environment of the babysitters' to their civilized odour-free homes, now tormented by the smells themselves, wondering what they would not give for a good warm traditional meal.

The cookers at Sixty-nine are on, full blast. Saucepans are bubbling, chappatis nest warmly under cloth covers, rice lies dormant and waiting. Whatever one thinks of the smells, it must be conceded that the inhabitants of Sixty-nine eat well. Chappatis and rice, vegetable, potato, and meat curries cooked the Goan, Madrasi, Hyderabadi, Gujarati, and Punjabi ways, channa the Caribbean way, fou-fou the West African way. Enough to make a connoisseur out of a resident, but a connoisseur of smells only because each group clings jealously to its own cuisine. And the experienced can tell, sniffing the air in the lobby, what Gulshan Bai's tiffin is today, for the sixth floor is a popular stop at this hour. So it is not unusual to find coming down in an elevator a well-dressed young couple looking stiffly in front, holding baby, baby's diaper bag, and the local version of a bundle that a Gujarati peasant might carry: a plastic bag around several plastic containers. Gulshan Bai's tiffin travels far.

In the evenings, neighbourhood boys gather to play street hockey or soccer around cars and over roundabouts and between pedestrians; cars pass at their own risk, boys play at theirs.

Out of this world Nurdin would wander in search of a job and return dejected, plunged into deeper despair. Sometimes he took daily jobs, invariably menial, loading and unloading with fellow Dar immigrants, and would come home and lie and say "filing," until that became a joke. Everyone knew what "filing" meant. Sometimes he simply refused to go out to these humiliations, watching game shows and talk shows at home, and joining the "A-T" crowd of idle men who met for chitchat and tea downstairs in the lobby in emulation of Dar's famous A-T Shop. On his idle days, in the afternoons he would clean up at home, sweeping away evidence of any degeneracy, giving the television time enough to cool. You could be sure that Fatima on one pretext or another, or when you were not looking, would detect any telltale residual warmth on its body. And when she did – did the girl show contempt already at this age?

Zera began to have trouble with jobs, which did not help matters. The job she had taken early on was as receptionist to a Chinese doctor. A perfect job, walking distance away, in the mall. She could do shopping during lunchtime. And after school the kids could play outside the office under her watchful eyes. But then, after a few months, she had been dismissed. "Your English," the doctor had said vaguely. A "Canadian" was duly installed. "I brought so many patients," she said. Which she had, and in revenge she soon sent word around that the doctor was unreliable.

Later she taught Gujarati, part time, at the Heritage Languages Program in a school, and money was scarce. Then a factory job came along, where her sister Roshan worked. But at this job, where she quality-checked sweatshirts and folded them for packing, there was a lot of dust and she had trouble breathing. She had dropped a hint after dinner once that making chappatis would not be such a bad idea. Fatima protested. Not only was the smell of concern, but also the dignity of the family. Nurdin suggested that there was not much difference in status between the two jobs. An argument ensued. A friendly argument, one of the first – and friendliest. Fatima, who went to school and spoke English with an accent neither of her parents could even move their mouths to imitate, now had a mind of her own. The chappati idea was dropped.

Zera, always fleshy, had put on more weight at an alarming rate. There were many among Don Mills' Dar immigrants who in their first three months of consuming potato chips and french fries and root beer simply burst out of the clothes they had come with. Happily for Nurdin, his wife, out of her sense of modesty, did not take to cutting her hair or wearing pants, as many other women started doing, regardless of the size of their buttocks. So there were homely women, who had always dressed in long frocks, suddenly emerging swinging immense hips clothed in brightly coloured acrylic pants, and you couldn't help looking and feeling ashamed at the same time.

For Zera, such questions of modesty were referred to the Master himself, Missionary, who reflected on values and tradition, and sent his verdict: If you wear pants, cover your behinds. An ardent request was submitted by Zera and his other former pupils, begging him to emigrate. We are desperate for guidance, they said. Life here is full of pitfalls. Children come home from school with questions we can't answer. And want to celebrate Christmas. They sent him a long list of innocent-looking items that contained pork by-products, from bread to toothpaste. What is a by-product? Please come. He was said to be considering.

On weekend evenings most Dar Shamsis went to the mosque, held at a school gym on Eglinton Avenue, a destination every bus driver on the 26 route had come to recognize, at which he would let off nervous newcomers whether the stop button had been pressed or not. The newcomer, gazing intently out of the window at familiar-looking people converging in small groups to a place he didn't quite know, would look up thankfully at the driver and step down with relief, spirits already soaring.

At the mosque a mukhi sat presiding from under a basketball ring. Here after prayers the newcomers announced themselves: tourists seeking spouses, jobs, ultimately reasons to stay; immigrants, en route to Calgary, Edmonton, or Vancouver, or simply staying in Toronto; visitors from south of the border. Once they had announced themselves the news would spread. So-and-so has come. What news from Dar? What price sugar? Do they mug you yet in the mosque in New York? And if they were staying in the city, the insurance agents would brace themselves, taking notes, keeping tabs – when the so-and-so's found a job, when an apartment. And finally some evening one of them would knock on the door – a former teacher perhaps, his own genial self, with all the authority of his old status, asking a thousand ifs – pointing out at once the virtues and the shaky foundations of this new existence. Insure, not against revolutions, but death.

On Saturday evenings after mosque, Nurdin and Zera would watch TV with the children. Or leaving them in the apartment, they would go up to the eighteenth floor to the open house, to watch people playing cards and to chitchat over tea, to find out the news in Dar – the status of roads and food prices and the dollar price – all, reassuringly, bad. And, perhaps, to meet "the boys," as Zera called them, the two new friends they had made, and if "the boys" were so inclined, to bring them home.

6

In the cavernous lobby of Sixty-nine, somewhat away from the path of the daily traffic, is a circular platform raised a foot and a half high, often used as a bench. In the centre, seated on a stool, a plaster goddess takes in with dumb composure all that goes on in the lobby, the comings and goings, the rendezvous, the daily battles with the elevators. Nude, long legged, her one hand rests purposely on her lap, the other raised to hold up something that's long been dislodged. She is, for all those who pass under her stony gaze, a real, if a little mysterious, presence. Her nose is bruised, giving her the look of an antique statue, and the white plaster of her substance has invited many a creative hand to improvise on her features with chalk and markers, which the successive supers have patiently tried to wipe clean, leaving instead a dull grey skin. The lap has enough room so that on a Friday or Saturday night you might see some drunk taking comfort. Sometimes the raised hand holds a flower or a book or an umbrella, other times something more private or obscene. And once a pious Hindu pressed the lady into the ranks of the gopis by placing beside her a brass statuette of the flute player, the gopi-seducer Krishna.

Under the neutral gaze of this Aphrodite or Lakshmi, some male inhabitants of Sixty-nine would gather in the mornings to discuss "life and politics," while their wives or mothers would be out at work or rolling chappatis upstairs in the apartments or, to be fair, out on their own breaks. This was the Don Mills A-T, men sitting in a circle on the goddess's platform, and standing around, sipping tea, sharing snacks, chatting.

At a little after nine in the morning Jamal would descend in an elevator, clutching close to him an old black briefcase. If you happened to be with him and wondered out loud, or silently with a sniff, to inquire where the smell of samosas was coming from this early in the morning, Jamal would give a louder sniff as rejoinder and agree forcefully: "These Pakis! Cooking twenty-four hours a day!" He might grin with his large mouth, brushing with his fingers his shiny black moustache in amusement. Altogether a friendly, not to say gregarious, fellow. One to begin conversations, not end them. Everyone at Sixty-nine knew him.

Jamal had been a lawyer back in Dar. More precisely, a junior but important constitutional expert in the government. Someone who had advised on the criminality of shady shopkeepers and corrupt cabinet ministers, helped to produce amendments and draft papers on emergency procedures, was now emerging from a Don Mills elevator, clutching the same briefcase that had hidden secrets of state but was now hiding samosas destined for sale at the nearest tuck-shop. The irony would be lost on Jamal, because for him there was new ground to conquer.

Jamal was the only son of a mathematics teacher who was part Persian and dreamt of a new Africa. In 1950, Jamal's father, influenced by the liberating optimism of the postwar era, founded a magazine of ideas called *Atom*. Its focus was the future, and its faith was the commonly espoused belief that Africa would in a few decades be like America. In one of its issues it favoured African independence, going so far as including on that subject an article by an African and another by an Indian from India. As if that was not enough, in a later issue the idea of racial integration was given serious thought. If the previous generation of pioneers could have intermarried or cohabited, so went the argument, what stopped the new generation from "mixing with our African brethren?" The community elders were perturbed, and so perhaps were the police. There was already some agitation by the Africans in neighbouring Kenya. It was suggested to Jamal the elder that perhaps the articles in his magazine should first be vetted by some committee so that nothing untoward or damaging was published. He should consider including recipes and jokes, brainteasers; the look of the magazine could surely be improved, there was money available. He refused. Thence began his downfall. A pretext was found to dismiss him from the community-run school: he did not have an education diploma. His decline was further aided by his own ineptness in all matters worldly. His wife took up support of the family, from which burden she found relief only after many years. *Atom* folded when its printer refused to donate his services any longer.

The boy Jamal (nicknamed "The Persian") was bright but misunderstood, an attention-getter, coarse and loud, tolerated by friends, an irritant to teachers. He could finish school only by going up-country, barely surviving two years of rigour away from the city. It says much for the final examination system, in which you simply put down your number on your paper and allowed yourself to be judged by anonymous examiners in Cambridge, that Jamal passed with flying colours the Higher School Certificate exam and was given a law scholarship by a ministry of education with no contact with the shop-keepers. The country was independent by then.

After finishing his degree he was recruited by the government. A brilliant political career surely lay ahead of him. He had already shone in student politics. He was outspoken, though charismatic and bright. He only had to play it right, to move up. But then the infamous nationalization of rental properties took place, the Great Betrayal that rocked the Asian community. Ways were now sought to mislead the government's grasping hand. Those who had despised his father came to him for his help. How they bowed and scraped before him, practically offered their daughters now, they who would not let him sit in their cars and would look to see if he had washed his feet when he came with their sons to their homes. And how Jamal had felt contempt at these cheap attempts to buy his influence.

One night, however, he received a phone call from a colleague warning him that a request for permission of his arrest was circulating in certain circles. Jamal did not wait to find out what, if anything, he had said or done. He fled overnight, at about the time the Lalanis were trying to obtain their Canadian visas. Jamal flew to Cuba, an attractive place for idealistic young men in those days. International politics intervened, however; he was not allowed to stay. He went to Brazil then, where he sold rugs for a year – in effect becoming a shopkeeper – and learned Portuguese, until his visa to go to Canada arrived.

By the time Jamal returned from the tuck-shop with his black briefcase now relieved of its oily contents, seated at the foot of the goddess, holding a mug of coffee and reading a magazine, would be Nanji, a former classmate. "What, reading the *Sun*?" Jamal would comment with a wide grin, and Nanji would look up with a smile from reading material far more serious. "So, what brief did you carry today?" would be his sarcastic reply.

Unlike Jamal's erratic and somewhat precarious academic career, Nanji's had been straightforward. School had conferred upon him also an identity based on his surname. Brilliant throughout, he had won a scholarship to a prestigious American university. Another brilliant career, it seemed, spawned at the same school by the same shopkeeper community. But the world had caught the community dreaming and ill-prepared as it now found its youth. From all the possible disciplines he could have chosen, Nanji picked a branch of linguistics in which there were not many jobs. So he taught an evening course at Woodsworth College and whiled away the rest of his time talking and reading.

His looks reflected his anxious nature. Tall, with a high forehead, sunken eyes, face marked with the remains of youthful acne, always in ill-fitting clothes. When the two former classmates met in Toronto after seven years, an instant friendship developed where once there had been contempt on one side and suspicion on the other. Jamal, outgoing, full of mischief, now waiting for a place in a Canadian law school while looking for women to take to bed, and tall, stern Nanji, with all the moral weight of the world on his shoulders, reading the existentialists and despairing.

"You know," Nanji told Jamal, in all earnestness, the first week they met, "the only choice, *real* choice, man has in the world is whether to go on living . . . or to commit suicide, end this absurd existence. Have you thought of that? Compared to this, all other questions are trivial, frivolous, irrelevant."

"Bana! Wow! You've hit me between the eyes, man. Who else could have thought of that!"

"It's not my original idea, I assure you," Nanji protested in embarrassment. Jamal, without the benefit of a liberal arts education, showed a naïveté sometimes that was simply unsettling, as unsettling as his commonsensical to-the-point reasoning.

"But suppose I use my free will to decide to go *on* with this absurd existence, as you call it. . . . "

"Well, if you really *choose* that . . . to go on living . . . then you live with that choice facing you every moment of your life. You are truly *alive*. Most people go on mindlessly of course, they don't *choose* to live. That's because they do what they are told or made to do. . . . And think of this: when death comes unasked, when it takes you by surprise, it will rob you of even this free choice, because when you thought you were choosing to live, *it* was only letting you live. The only way you can exercise free will, defeating *it*, is by taking your own life."

All this in utmost seriousness.

Jamal grinned. "My friend, you don't see many philosophers exercising their free will!"

Nanji smiled. "Well, they say that the body has a greater desire to live than the mind to perish."

"Wow!"

Questions of morality and ethics, of good faith and compromise tormented Nanji. Suppose you were walking on a road and saw on a side street a person being attacked. What would you do, risk your life or that of the other person? Questions that, to Jamal at least, had a simple answer: save the person you can be sure of saving, yourself, and try to save the other by fetching help. But there was an idealism in the other, a death instinct perhaps, that refused this cold-blooded utilitarian logic. Suppose a girl was being raped, he would say. And then torment himself further by asking himself, Why this obsession with rape? What sins, evil desires, was he covering up? *All existences make me anxious, from the smallest fly to the mysteries of Incarnation. . . .*

"It seems," he told Jamal, "that to become westernized, which is what we've opted for by coming here, we have to go back and battle by battle relive all their battles – spiritual struggles. How can you otherwise assimilate generations of experience – only now we've reached the Age of Reason. . . ."

"But isn't that better, Nanji? Our God is not dead, we are better off – "

"Can we survive here, with our God . . . can *He* survive?"

So the two constantly discussed questions of life and death, at least to Nanji, Jamal often sceptical but egging him on. For Jamal was affected less by the contents of the thought than by the process itself: to be discussing with someone so obviously qualified as

Nanji thrilled him. "Wait," he would promise, "when I've made my millions I will have all the intellectuals like you and artists and musicians around me, my own durbar where you don't have to worry about mundane things like where your next meal is going to come from. . . . "

At the foot of the goddess, now, others would arrive and join in the conversation, which naturally flowed into more jolly directions. The A-T was in session. Tea would be fetched, and samosas. Among the men here there was an unspoken democracy, regardless of education, age, and social background. The former bandmaster Ramju would arrive from the fourteenth floor for a break from the chappatis, leading two noisy toddlers in a march, out for an ostensible walk, which their parents demanded. Ramju would sit on the pedestal and the children would run around the lobby, under his stern bloodshot eyes, and whenever they got into a fight or started to cry, he would shout at them "Shaddup!" And the two toddlers would reply "Shaddup! Shaddup!"

At first the Lalanis took Nanji for a simple young man, from a small town perhaps. He seemed shy. Nurdin even asked him if they were hiring where he worked. He had politely said no, realizing the reason why they had invited him to lunch. "What factory do you work at?" Nurdin asked, and Nanji had painfully cleared his throat, blood rushing to his face. "Oh, I work at the University of Toronto. Part time, of course."

"Wow! said Fatima. "Do you teach there?"

"Yes."

"Wow! Are you a professor or something?"

"Sort of. Part time."

"Wow."

Nurdin and Zera exchanged an embarrassed look and then tried to appear interested in his work, as he helped them change the subject.

It did inflame Nanji sometimes the way he was taken for a labourer and even a shopkeeper. He should not have mentioned the incident to Jamal, but he did, and Jamal, the next time he saw Nurdin, said to him, "So, Nurdin, we hear you want to be a professor." And Nurdin suffered that jibe, fending it off as best as he could by laughing with the rest.

But they came to love Nanji for his simplicity and his humility and that helpless, lost look he bore. When they fed him, he ate well, with relish, cleaning his plate, while he answered the questions with which all four plied him. They were sure he was a lonely young man – and a hungry one as well.

In Zera he brought forth a mixture of maternal and sisterly feelings. "Make this your home," she had said, and he had consented gratefully. When he hadn't shown his face for a few days, she would fret, and worry lest she did anything to make her partiality to him known to his friend, Jamal. Because

Jamal, she told Nurdin, is like a dormant snake – walk carefully when near him, he cannot help striking. Best of all, for her, she could talk religion with Nanji. He was an agnostic, almost. He had reached this path through study and thought, by opening the door to doubt, so that quite naturally religious questions interested him. In all these discussions, Nanji never professed a faith or showed piety, discussing clinically yet showing such intimate knowledge of the faith. Perhaps his lost, innocent look suggested piety to his hosts. On the other hand Zera was no fool and surely guessed that Nanji did not practise, but anyone who spent so much time thinking and reading about religion was, must be, religious.

The two children loved him. "Finally," said Fatima one day, "I know someone here – two people" – she took note of Jamal – "that I can respect. Isn't that something?" Much to the consternation of her mother. Fatima's two heroes had been "out there" in the world, had been accepted there, they had independent views, could explain the world to her. No reverting to Swahili and making silly jokes she did not find funny, about the differences between "back there" and "out here." Nanji was also a playmate and companion to her and Hanif; he taught them how to play imaginary cricket, using only a pencil, and chess and backgammon, and went to the library and the Science Centre with them, buying them hamburgers and pizza without converting dollars to shillings in his mind. So taken was she with this young man whose only pants were Levi's that she swore she would never wear dresses.

Nurdin watched this infatuation with a twinge of envy: what dreams you dream when they are babies. But how can you feel jealous of an educated, respectable young man taking your children under his wing? He was like a younger brother – and don't all children fall in love with their uncles? That was Zera's opinion, and she must be right. Better this than the wrong kind of influence. Drugs and whatnot.

And hadn't *they* taken *him* in, Nurdin could have argued with himself. So much so as even to try and find him a wife. "Why not get married?" Zera once said, making it sound like a good idea just come to mind. "No," he replied, "no marriage for me," and received the full vocal support of Fatima. Zera was not satisfied. "It is not possible," she said. "There must be someone, there must be something." She broached the subject with Jamal: "What if I introduce a nice girl to your friend? Educated, you know, but not too much. Plain, like him." "Cool it," said Jamal. "You'll kill him. Besides" – he let drop – "there is someone in New York."

From then on, in Nanji's presence, Zera would make teasing remarks about New York, and he would blush. "It's not that simple . . ." he would begin.

7

"When does a man begin to rot?" Gazing at the distant CN Tower blinking its signals into the hazy darkness, Nurdin asked himself the question. He sat in his armchair, turned around to look out into the night. Through the open balcony the zoom of the traffic down below in the valley was faintly audible, as was the rustle of trees. Pleased with the sound of his silent question, he repeated it in his mind again, this time addressing the tower. The lofty structure he had grown familiar with over the months, from this vantage point, and he had taken to addressing it. "When does a man begin to rot?" he asked. Faithful always, it blinked its answer, a coded message he could not understand.

He liked to keep the room darkened when alone. Somewhat vaguely he was aware of the photograph on the wall, on his right. Vaguely, because he rarely looked at it, and when he did, by accident, he tried as much as possible to block his father's face on it from his mind. Something had changed, he did not know what, perhaps new ideas, like the question he was asking, not knowing why. Some inner reserve was creaking, shifting its weight. The photograph on the wall, its face, intruded into his consciousness at this moment, eyes boring into him from the side, and he shuddered.

His father's photograph, taken in the 1940s, was one of the prized possessions Zera had brought from Dar. Other things had seen the dustbins – photographs, old books, souvenirs – but not this. It was the first object to go up on the walls. Sometimes when she lighted incense sticks and went around the apartment consecrating it, she would stand before the photograph and hold the incense to it – as one would to a real person – thus giving it a real presence in the home. The fez on the small head, the bushy eyebrows, the hard eyes, the small mouth: relentless in judgement here as the real person had been in Africa.

"Do you have lewd thoughts?" he asked Nanji one evening. Nanji had squirmed and grunted, and Nurdin pressed on: "No, seriously." Then from the kitchen had come Zera's "Be ashamed of yourself, Nurdin," saving Nanji's day.

What did the younger man see in him, he had often wondered. The answer was close at hand: a simpleton, one to bear life's drudgeries. Truth to tell, this was not far from his own estimation of himself, but he would have added "good-natured." He was shrewd enough, he thought, to know what was what; he just lacked that something that would take him far, in business, for example. He had never had it, he accepted that, and he had let his father arrange his life for him, even though he had had inklings of what he really might have liked. It had been simple, life in the family, the community, so long as you did not question it. Few did; it was not worth the trouble, brought you nothing. There were a few accepted paths to take, and that was that. Somehow or other you fitted in, with your strengths and your weaknesses. And before you knew it you were worrying about your children, and after that, the fate of your soul in the first life, as it was called.

Barring a few phantoms of thoughts, he had been satisfied. But now he felt tremors of change inside him, and new yearnings.

He had seen much of Nanji recently, had toyed with the idea of sitting down with him, having a serious discussion, perhaps bare his soul, show the rot setting in. He didn't have the courage for that.

He didn't have the words for it, the right approach.

What do they know of our weaknesses, these youngsters, so surefooted in their rarefied world . . . seeing us solid as rocks – and as dumb. When all the time there exist thoughts, lurk desires inside you which you dare not look at, making lewd gestures at you to catch attention and you walk away, heart beating like a shy schoolgirl. . . . Only now all the murk there threatens to surface and the rock threatens to fall apart.

Perhaps he would rot physically first. He felt tired these days, old. His hair had greyed and thinned, there were lines on his face, and his skin somehow looked more opaque in the mirror. How old was he? Forty-six, about the average life expectancy where he was born, but here in Canada you got an extended lease on life.

The closest Nurdin found to a sales job since he was turned down for the position in Eatons' shoe department was the midnight shift at a donut store on Spadina Avenue. What had made him expect a sales job – "something managerial," he had said to Zera – in these dismal hours he could never after understand. Desperation, bluster . . . he had stated his knowledge of accounts on the application form, and the man who took it from him had looked suitably impressed.

It was a disaster from his first step inside. He found himself working under a tough-looking elderly woman who answered his shy grin with a crusty "Go inside and put on a jacket." And as he came to the counter wearing the yellow jacket, feeling a little low and degraded in this uniform that was stiff and odorous with the sweat of previous wearers, he was handed a ball of wet cloth and told to wipe the tables. A girl, rather pretty, also worked there. She liked him even less. November cold had driven idlers inside and the place was crowded; smoke and vapour saturated the air, together with odours of cream, stale donuts, and cigarette stubs; a group of permanent-looking hangers-on sat at a few tables, discussing vigorously what must surely have been politics, in a foreign language over foreign-looking newspapers. East Europeans, he gathered, having heard that there were many in Toronto. The girl apparently was also one of them.

Nurdin soon realized that the two women regarded him as nothing more than a servant, keeping him as far as possible from the counter where they sat chatting when not serving. This was not the job he'd come for. He debated over and over with himself whether to stay the shift or go back home, but without resolution until the showdown came when the woman asked him to take the mop. He refused. He simply took a cup of coffee, picked up a plain donut, and sat down.

The woman came and stood in front of him. "All right," she said. "Scram before I call the cops." Nurdin looked at her. "You've not paid for these," she said. He stood up and left.

It was cold and windy outside, and miserably he realized that the subways must have already stopped for the night. He walked up to Bloor Street, looking for another place to go in and sit. He found that he still had on the uniform jacket of the donut store. He did not have the heart to throw it away, so he folded it and placed it outside a building entrance. Fortunately there was another donut store two blocks away on Bloor. The girl there eyed him but let him stay. Later on, with very few customers present, she came and placed a cup of coffee in front of him, and still later a magazine called *The Real Truth*. He glared at it between the snatches of sleep he couldn't resist as he waited out the night. When daylight came, he went out, after shaking the girl awake to say his thanks (to which she merely nodded sleepily), and took the subway home.

He had tried out as a temporary security guard. Surely nothing more than a watchman, he admitted, but still. His first assignment was at a new building in Scarborough where not a bus passed by. When, after a walk of half an hour from the nearest bus stop, he arrived two hours late, there was somebody else present, a tall handsome Asian man with a moustache, who treated him no better than a thief. And so, a long walk back to the bus stop.

Even as a lowly parking-lot attendant he had

had no luck. After only a few months he was summarily dismissed one evening, together with all the other attendants, by a supervisor who told him, "You are either dumb or too clever. Either way I don't want you." Only at the A-T gathering in the lobby of Sixty-nine, when he told them, "I say, the strangest thing . . . " was it explained to him how one could make extra money as a parking-lot attendant and how not to get caught.

The A-T was of course a regular source of information on employment and immigration. Nurdin was told there how he could get a job as subway-car cleaner at night, working with some of the other fellows of Sixty-nine. The job was easy. You just did a few cars and then found an isolated one where you played cards for the remainder of the night. How do you get such a job? You simply had to "oil the hands" of the supervisor. "What-what?" he said, incredulous. "Here? In Canada?" "Tell him, Uncle," someone said. And they all turned to look at the man they called Uncle, a stout, elderly former businessman, who spoke the wisdom of experience. "Yes. Just give your first week's salary."

Notch by notch it seemed to Nurdin he had come down in self-esteem and expectation, grasping whatever odd job came his way, becoming a menial in the process. Back home even your glass of water was brought by a servant. A servant to fetch you from school, to hold your bag. Things had changed there, of course, but not that much. And now, here. In Canada. He had carried cases on his back the likes of which he would have thought he could not even move an inch; he had pressed trousers, cooked french fries, swept and mopped floors. You could weep. But the children wanted a car, a brand-new Chevy, to go to Wasaga Beach, Niagara Falls, Buffalo. And mosque, how could you go by bus to mosque: where all comparisons begin and end, where your real worth is measured. When did you arrive? You tell them. What work do you do? And you're crushed, what to tell them. All the while newcomers, younger people, find jobs, success stories proliferate, bus and subway drivers in uniforms – men you thought no better than you – haughtily stare you down, prouder than doctors and accountants with cute kids and expensive wives. But whatever job you did you had to show the basics, the stars earned in this new country.

8

On the dark green wall behind the plaster goddess in the lobby of Sixty-nine there used to hang two large paintings in garish colours, in crude wooden frames that could have been the product of a beginner at a prison workshop. Both were the work of one hand, even a casual observer could have noted that. Vague human figures, in what looked like kneeling positions in one of them; in the other a person with arms stretched out as if crucified or simply flying; masks looked on at whatever tragedy was going on, and everything merged into a background done in coarse strokes in colours that could have been inspired by the leaden green of the wall. If they had not been obtained without cost, they would not have been there. But one morning the residents emerging from the elevators on their way out noticed that the paintings were gone. Two great rectangular patches marked the places they had occupied. It was surmised that they had been taken the previous night. Who would steal those dark paintings whose absence was now so strongly felt that complaints had even gone to the superintendent? There was a report by some of the ladies who go to mosque at five in the morning that the super himself had overseen their removal in the small hours of dawn. There the matter rested.

These paintings were the work of a resident who had since left. Why they came to be done can be traced to a single incident in the recent history of this once stolid city which was now feeling its own winds of change.

At 8:20 one spring evening, Nanji had given his class their midterm test, and now stood with the test papers in one hand at the streetcar stop on the corner of College and St. George streets. Characteristically, head lowered, shoulders sagging, he was thinking of one student in particular. A big-bosomed tall girl with remarkably distinguished features – aristocratic was the word that came to mind. Patrician. Why aristocratic – is there such a thing? Nothing plain about that face – notice she uses no makeup, nothing obvious – it could have come, that face, from a long line of careful breeding. A high, prominent forehead;

every feature on that face distinct and prized; smooth skin. Flawless. And the long gold-brown hair. There was a casualness to her clothes that was studied, expensive, there was that ease in her manner, an assurance, that suggested security. A secure past and a secure future. She had a way of making herself noticed, he had observed, by coming to him and asking questions, however trivial, and being satisfied by whatever he said. Not a stupid girl, because some of the questions were sharp. A girl like her, nothing can go wrong with her. In a few years she'll be in Rosedale, running respectable charities, wife of a Bay Street executive. Would this one, so friendly and deferential now, calling him "professor" and "sir," even notice or acknowledge him then . . . and if she did, on what terms?

His students calling him "sir" and coming around him to ask questions after class had Jamal simply bowled over one evening. Jamal had come in to town with him on some pretext and then hung around him, making it impossible for him to gather his thoughts before class. And then, as he gave his lecture, Jamal sat in, high above in the last corner seat, drawing attention every conceivable way. He was irrepressible, a comic foil to Nanji's high seriousness. He would look deeply interested, apparently hanging on to every word of the professor, and then sit back to grin at him familiarly, as if to say, "Ah, my friend, how good you look! How far you've come!" Once he exclaimed, quite audibly, "Ah!" so as not to let a fine point escape his approval or the notice of everyone else present. Jamal might as well have been sitting at a qawali recital, where such outbursts of approval are appreciated. Nanji could have exploded with frustration. And finally, as if that was not enough, on two occasions Jamal even attempted to start a discussion: "I can see that, sir, but don't you think in the Bantu languages you have an exception there . . . because of the long isolation," looking tremendously earnest and talking completely out of context. After the lecture Nanji told him, "Never again." But Jamal had been impressed, and it was good to have impressed him, because Jamal would go far.

Nanji was smiling grimly at his own cynicism when the streetcar arrived. He got in and remained seated alone all the way, even when most of the seats were taken and some passengers stood. This happened often to him. Racism, the word kept intruding into his mind and he kept pushing it back. On what basis racism? It could be my face, dark, brooding, scowling, cratered. Perhaps I look like a bum. Professor Nanji? What we have become: suspecting racism, but never certain, touchy as a raw wound, blaming innocent people and letting the guilty walk smugly away because you can never be quick enough with a reply. Feeling angry and frustrated afterwards. I should have said this, if only I had said it . . . the next time. . . .

He got off at the College subway station. Inside, he stood by himself on the dimly lighted platform, well away from the draft of the staircase. The trains were slow that evening, a fair number of people had collected on the platform. Later he would not be able to remember what he had been thinking of, waiting those first few minutes for the train. Memory began with the picture in his mind of three youths running down the stairs mock-fighting with each other, big, in jackets, their boots grating on the gritty floor. Two had crew-cut hair, blond, the third wore a funny hat. In Nanji's teachers' vocabulary: three louts.

One of the blond-haired louts was obviously the leader – there was a style, a control (or pretence of it) in his gestures; the funny-hatted one, cackling at every opportunity, was a sidekick. The people on the platform instinctively moved away, giving the youths' antics more room. The effect of this movement was that of forming a loose circle around them. Perhaps the youths became conscious of this circle, the attitude it reflected; they stood up, defiant, threatening; the circle loosened some more, now with apprehension. But to no avail, they had smelled blood and they struck, baiting the bystanders with taunts and sarcasm. Only youth can appropriately respond to youth. The victims here were mostly older. Mercifully the attackers kept flitting, prancing away. The youths were some distance from Nanji, there were people between. He was aware of their movements, could hear their grating menace, and he was terribly afraid lest through some magnetism he lead them to his direction; his heart beating wildly, pushing back a prayer because he had stopped believing in prayers. Please, not here, let them stop, let a train come. . . .

The subway tunnels were as dark and endless as a moonless, starless sky. From time to time he swept a glance up and down the platform, pausing briefly to watch the three louts. Once they stopped defiantly in front of a stout lady going home with a package, then in front of a clean-cut young man with a brief-case. They walked up to a young woman, but were less abusive, perhaps because she laughed with them, perhaps because they saw her as closer to their age and background.

During one of these furtive surveys he saw someone he knew, Esmail, standing at the edge of the platform, looking nervously for a train to come. Es-mail, a little over average height, looking taller for the thick-soled shoes, which many Dar men wore for that purpose, and in a very conspicuous beige Kaunda suit, which they had all bought in a frenzy of African patriotism in Dar but now wore proudly in Toronto to set themselves apart. Esmail, also resi-dent at Sixty-nine Rosecliffe, was a man of few words. He would be returning from the bakery where he worked, carrying in the package in his hand, presumably, the meat pies he himself had baked.

Nanji began an instinctive step towards his compatriot, but then realized he would draw atten-tion and stopped. At that moment a shiver ran down his spine. The three louts had come up behind Es-mail and began their abuse. "Paki!" one of them shouted joyfully. Esmail turned towards them, look-ing frightened. "What do you have there, Paki? Hey,

hey? Paki-paki-paki. . . ." They leered, they jeered, crowding in on him in front, behind him the subway tracks. Bystanders looked away, embarrassed, uncomfortable. It was clear that unless a train quickly came here would begin and end the main mischief of the bullies. A heavy, oppressive feeling overcame Nanji. He wanted to run to Esmail's aid, to shout at the impassive people to do something, to call the police, to raise the alarm . . . but his legs didn't move, his mouth didn't open. He would make himself stare at the spectacle of three big youths bullying a cowering man, a man he knew, then he would look away, in a mixture of shame and fear, hoping that when his eyes moved back again the ordeal would be over.

Perhaps Esmail had answered them back, or perhaps his silence simply goaded the gloating, prancing youths beyond control. Because at some point Nanji became aware of shouting and pandemonium, the youths shouting, pounding up the stairs and out of the station. An alarm was raised, and suddenly people were gathered where Esmail had stood – but they were looking down onto the tracks.

Esmail, punched in the stomach, had been thrown down and was crying in horrible, pathetic moans, "Save me, save me, I have done nothing." People shouted encouragements: "Get up! Stand up!" But Esmail couldn't get up. An attendant arrived, then two policemen from the street. Brakes screeched somewhere along the tracks in a tunnel, in which a light was now visible. An ambulance arrived, Esmail was removed, taken away on a stretcher.

Nanji went home numb, depressed. The whole brutal incident was shocking, the more so for being wanton and racial, directed at someone who could have been himself. In that very real sense, he too had been attacked. What ached now, and horribly, was the recollection of his own behaviour during the attack. He had not moved an inch, not uttered a syllable, to defend the man. True, neither had anyone else – but what of his idealism, the long hours he had spent formulating it? He had fallen into the hole he had himself dug, setting standards impossible for an ordinary person to follow . . . and he was a very ordinary man where physical courage was concerned. He was a coward. Until now, what he had suffered was pleasurable pain, an indulgence, a luxury of the idle because he could *talk* of choice. Now he knew he could never make the choice, but simply go on. And the moral standard he had set for himself, through hypothetical examples, he had failed, not out of cold-bloodedness but out of cowardice. He wished Jamal had been there. Jamal would have known how to act, he would have *acted*. Because there was more to the cruelty and rough edge in Jamal, there was also the hot blood of instinct. Jamal would have been roused to an act of courage. Jamal was life, he, Nanji, was death.

In his apartment he sat down on his bed and wept tears of regret, of shame, of hopelessness. Where have we come, what are we becoming? He wished she were with him, the girl, his nemesis in New York, whom he wryly referred to as "she." To regain his composure, he made himself some coffee.

Nanji's parents had both died in a famous accident when he was very young. They had joined a marriage jaan, a procession on the groom's side, all the way from Dar to Mombasa by bus, leaving the boy with his grandmother. A happy, lively bus, ringing with song and merriment, full of new clothes and spices and nuts and gold jewellery. To get into Mombasa town, the ferry which had to be taken capsized. All sixty passengers and the driver drowned. Only some of the bodies were recovered – the waters were shark-infested. For days loose items of clothing, luggage, or other belongings were washed ashore, which some families used in burial ceremonies. The community was cut deep by the accident, so many families were affected. Nanji's parents were among those not found.

This was the tragedy buried deep in his memory, which he only rarely invoked. It was something he could not look back on. In any case, he did not have many memories with his parents in them – something he could only turn away from to look ahead. Hence the new schools that were opened in Dar, and the new public library, had occupied him completely. His grandmother did not demand anything from him, as she lived on a pension. But he had to be with her when he could, that was obvious to him. So he had grown up, the silent brooding type.

When he went to California to study, his grandmother first lived alone, then with one of her sons. It was while Nanji was away that she died; then the great nationalizations back home, and before he knew it half the community was in Canada. He was alone, adrift and floating.

At university he underwent a major transformation. The war was on in Vietnam. He arrived immediately after the great student riots of the late sixties at Kent State and Ohio State, Chicago, Berkeley, Columbia, and Harvard. It was fall, leaflets abounded on the campus announcing a multitude of movements and meetings. What struck him in those early days was the sheer number, the tumult of beliefs, thought systems that seemed to make up America. He realized he could think, should think, on every conceivable issue in the world. He was *of* the world. His was a modest path, reading Nehru and Gandhi, catching up on Indian nationalism, a subject unknown to the colonial Dar syllabuses. Then Hanoi was bombed, and a strike called. Students wearing red bands picketed and chanted, holding hands in solidarity. He had crossed several picket lines, between classes, until a demonstrator once challenged him: "Why don't you join?" That he could have joined he had never realized, until then. I am against the war, he reasoned. If one side stops it, the other side is not going to start a massacre. He did not cut classes, but every day for a few hours he joined the picket lines, expressing an opinion. Once, under an astute leader, the demonstration simply found itself marching and took over the ROTC building for the night. Nanji was there and appeared in the photo in the student paper the next day. Later from Gandhiism to a loss of faith, and to replace that, the constant search, which is what living had become for him.

He met *her*, the girl whom he would later refer to as "she," at a party in New York. He lived in Boston then. Shy as he was, he found himself obliged to escort her back to her apartment. A friendship had been struck and they had taken to visiting each other. She was so flighty, as he thought then, so superficial in everything. But that was the key: everything. She would do everything if she could, just to be doing it, not out of a special interest or passion. Like Jamal, she lived with a vengeance, which is why she attracted so many people around her. Unlike Jamal, though, she lacked bite, which made you feel protective towards her. She seemed so fragile, ever since that moment he insisted on accompanying her home, and upstairs to her door, after the party.

She had delighted in him, sensing in him the genuine article. She took him around, in spite of his diffidence, to parties, to people he would never have dreamed of meeting. Everyone – their friends – knew, accepted: Yasmin and Nanji belonged together. But for them, him and her, there was closeness, there were tender moments and mutual concern, no more. Not for her anyway, she couldn't be drawn closer, skating away expertly into her busy world of fashionable people. So that every time they parted, every time for a few weeks, he would be in pieces, swearing not to call her, not to see her again, until the next time she called, and his resolve evaporated. They developed their own peculiar brand of friendship.

He had come to Toronto almost by chance. He had obtained his immigrant visa on a trip to Vancouver, automatically, as a citizen of a Commonwealth country, and had not been aware of his new status until Canada was in the news and someone asked him to check. So that the visa would remain valid, he came to Toronto. And stayed. Once on his way to New York, his name was punched into a computer by U.S. Immigration. He was, it was discovered, an undesirable alien. His student days had caught up with him. So he could not go back to New York, at least not on days when he was checked up on. His visits became less frequent. He had not seen her for more than a year, had not heard from her for several months. Meanwhile she had become his "she," not a name with a face and figure but a composite of emotion and memory, dormant for now but ready to explode. His last phone call to her had ended awkwardly and abruptly. She was obviously busy with her social schedule, and he had no trouble imagining it.

Having finished his coffee, and calmed himself somewhat, Nanji went to the Lalanis'.

The family had just sat down to watch the news. A place was made for him, as a matter of course, but he remained standing and said, "Have you heard – about Esmail?" His manner suggested something ghastly had happened, to himself, so that he was made to sit down and receive Zera's ministrations. He told them what had happened, and Zera telephoned Esmail's apartment. Esmail's sister, with whom he lived, knew of the incident, in fact people had already begun to arrive to show sympathy. Zera could hear them in the background. Hanif and Fatima were told to stay home, and the three adults walked up two flights of stairs to join the sympathizers.

There were people from all the neighbourhood buildings, some thirty in number. How had they all heard in such a short time? The sofa and chairs had been moved to the walls and were all occupied. More people sat on the floor. They looked like mourners gathered in the first hours after news of death – with uneasy sighs and subdued murmurs and sympathetic glances towards the next of kin, the sister sitting in a prominent place, distraught and tearful, flanked by solicitous relations.

They seemed to be waiting, for something, for someone, to break the tension. Waiting and thinking: What now? Was this a sign of things to come . . . danger to self and property, to wife and kids. Have we come to the right place after all. In all these years in Africa not to have seen anything so wanton, so arbitrary, so public. If they had wanted money, yes.

Anything political, yes, riots, yes, they were understandable. But this, public humiliation, by kids. And where had they learned this hatred? Not from their parents? not from their elders? – that was hard to imagine. How can you send the children to school, to play, to the supermarket, how can you let the girls out?

From the corridor came Jamal's voice, nothing tentative about it, and welcome as the tinkle of ice on a hot day. He entered, in a black suit and red tie, tall and handsome, just in from a late rendezvous, and instantly anticipatory eyes full of unanswered questions turned to him. Jamal sensed the unspoken honour and braced himself. Slowly and deliberately he walked up to Esmail's sister and put his hand on her shoulder.

"Don't worry. Your brother will go down in history. His suffering will not have been in vain. He is the first and last. From now on we will fight back!" His voice had risen in pitch. Jamal had addressed many student rallies in Dar, as Nanji recalled.

"Aré, man, we are not Sikhs, you know." This from the clown who is always present at such meetings.

"The blacks kicked us out, now the whites will do the same. . . . Where do we go from here?"

"Looks like Pakistan for us."

"There are worse goons there. Did you hear of the two murders – "

A woman cut in impatiently. "Why doesn't someone tell these Canadians we are not Pakis. I have never been to Pakistan, have you been to Pakistan? Tell them we are East Africans!"

"You tell them."

"Aré," Jamal's voice came in derision, "it is because of milksops like you that we have to suffer such ignominy. Your time has come and gone. The blacks fingered your asses and you let them. We will fight back."

A fight would have erupted right there if the counsel of the women had not prevailed, and if that excellent soother of nerves, masala tea, not been produced.

It was past one o'clock before the meeting ended, when an elderly female relation simply stood up and said, "Now everyone go."

Esmail had broken both shins, but he would live.

When he heard the story, surprisingly, Jamal expressed no contempt for Nanji's lack of initiative. In order to discuss the incident, for there was much on their minds, they had taken a stroll on Rosecliffe Park Drive. It was a cool, starry night. Except for themselves, and the odd car, the street was empty. The solitude drew them closer, into a communion they had never known before. Their voices, though controlled, rang clear in the open space.

"Scared shitless, were you?" Jamal said.

"Yes."

"The bastards. You know, it burns me up."

"What – "

"You know that Somerset Arms girl?"

"The manager?" The woman in question was quite a few years older than Jamal.

"Yes, the bloody manageress."

"Well?"

"She's spurned me all this while. 'You give me the creeps,' she told me. But now she's giving me the eye."

Nanji was silent. Jamal's sexual escapades did not really interest him.

"You see it was Kassam who was fucking her meanwhile," Jamal muttered on.

"Oh, and now they've broken up."

Jamal looked furtively around him. Nothing moved. "You want to know what really happened? If I tell you, don't tell anyone."

"Except the rest of the world, you mean. Go on."

"You know Kassam – Gorilla? Here's what he says to me, listen: 'I had just finished fucking this woman. We were lying on our backsides, smoking, and I was thinking what a wonderful world this is, if I had to give up everything for this, it's been worth it.' What's he given up, except the jungle! Now listen, Nanji. This is Gorilla: 'Then this gauri who's been oohing and aahing me, she turns her flank to put out her cigarette and she says to me, "Why do you Pakis come to this country?" Just like that. I had been getting up to pee, Jamal, and I just burned up inside. I was halfway out of bed, but I simply let her have it.' "

"What – you mean – " said an open-mouthed Nanji to Jamal, who was doubled over in soundless laughter.

"He peed on her, man. 'This is what we Pakis are going to do to you,' he said."

"Don't tell me, you plan to do the same thing," said Nanji.

Jamal, almost recovered, brought his hands together in a silent clap.

But Nanji was impressed. Not at the exhibition but at the sheer energy and anger expressed. Some of his compatriots would move mountains if they didn't aim so low.

9

The incident at the Yonge and College subway station marked a new beginning in the lives of the Dar immigrants. For one thing, the outrage expressed officially, though perhaps too piously, by police, newspapers, and ordinary citizens decided once and for all that the line had been overstepped, that this was beyond tolerable limit. Toronto the Good would not have it. It brought home, to everybody, the fact that the immigrants were here to stay, they could not, would not, simply go away.

The incident had such an effect that afterwards some would attribute to it the small but perceptible rise in car sales. Immigrants, if they could afford it, and sometimes even when they couldn't, simply stopped using public transport. Many seized on the aftermath of this well-publicized incident to begin a new career – that of selling cars – and you could see more and more of the jolly-faced salesmen on the community TV channel on Sunday exhorting in a multitude of accents.

Esmail took a long time to recover. But he became an instant celebrity. His photos appeared in all the newspapers, depicting various stages of his recovery. There were even photos, in a feature article, from his childhood. In hospital he was showered with gifts and goodwill messages from many communities. When he was discharged the entire staff on duty came to see him off. When he returned in a wheelchair to Sixty-nine a welcome sign greeted him, under which, surrounded by other well-wishers, stood the local MPP and a local representative from the Asian community – none other than Jamal, whose idea it had been to invite the politician. During the following weeks, Esmail was deluged by visitors, bringing words of comfort and reassurance, bearing presents of all kinds, and even envelopes stuffed with money. All this culminated in a major demonstration that turned into quite a fête, and a salutory lesson for Jamal.

It was a warm late-spring day, a Sunday, and a large number of Asians, many of them prominent, met around noon at the school on Rosecliffe Park Drive. Teachers, professors, doctors, and government employees, most of them alien to Rosecliffe Park. To the Dar people, in the buildings just across from the school, the event came as a surprise, even though announcements had been posted in English and Gujarati. But who reads posters? For them the important news was read out in the mosque, then travelled by word of mouth for those who missed mosque. On that bright Sunday afternoon they finally got wind of the rally – Rosecliffe Park Drive had become a promenade with unfamiliar faces, posters flew about – and they took note of it, but warily. A Paki rally was not really their cup of tea – weren't they from Africa? A few of them went to the meeting, to see what it was all about. It seemed that they were being forced into an identity they didn't care for, by the media and public, and now by these Paki Asians who meant well but couldn't keep their distance. None of them seemed to realize, or care, that Esmail belonged to them, their particular East African Asian Shamsi community.

The meeting had been called for by an ad hoc group of successful Asian immigrants setting themselves up as leaders of the community. It was well organized but, initially, tedious. A communiqué had been drawn up and was read out. No one beyond the first few rows heard it, and there were grumbles. It was read out again, then one more time when the janitor of the building had been discovered, the headmaster telephoned, and the PA system brought out. Speeches followed. Just when rival factions from the floor began vying for attention, Esmail was

opportunely wheeled in, and received a standing
ovation. He said a few emotional words and gave up,
tearful, and received once more a standing ovation. A
demonstration had been planned and, since it had to
go somewhere, Esmail was quickly wheeled away to
the gate of Sixty-nine to await it. There followed a
rally the likes of which Don Mills had never seen.
Several hundred people – including children – of all
backgrounds, smiling, chanting, carrying provoca-
tive placards: ESMAIL WE ARE WITH YOU, NO TO
APARTHEID, LET MY PEOPLE COME. At the gate they
stopped. They filled the driveway, overflowed onto
the sidewalk, the road, and the parkette across from
it. Esmail was presented with a cheque.

With clapping and cheering the demo finally
came to an end, the crowd gradually diffusing. Ice
cream and hot dog vans appeared, the sun had kept
faith, as Nanji might have put it, and music was in
the air. There and then another small meeting got
under way in the parkette. This one drew together
the intellectual and artistic left wing, many of them
known to Nanji through his university connections.
It was a lively gathering and many stood by to watch.

A witty young man had been set up as emcee.
His hair was gathered at the back of his head in a
net, which created the effect of a black beanbag and
bobbed up and down when he spoke, giving him a
humorous aspect. After opening remarks, he introduced a soft-spoken bearded man in a suit, puffing at
a pipe, who gave a short chatty talk about the impor-
tance of fighting racism at all levels, beginning with

the schools and textbooks. Then a woman in sari, much loved it seemed, was gently pushed to the centre and she gave a personal account of discrimination. She was a single mother, and she, too, it turned out, had been confronted in a subway station. She ended by reading a poem about the experience, then two more poems in encore. Then the emcee read his own humorous poetry, poking fun at the government and what he called "multivulturalism." Then a heavily built Jamaican woman performed dub poetry. The gathering became calm and the bystanders moved closer to listen better, utterly captivated by the rhythm, the strange yet recognizable sounds, the enchanting defiance. There was loud applause, ending the event with an explosive climax. The left wing, it seemed, had stolen the show.

Magically, a bookstall had appeared on the sidewalk and then a samosa stand beside it, manned by Ramju, the former bandmaster and now chappati-helper of the fourteenth floor of Sixty-nine. An artist, a short fierce-looking sculptor with a Lenin beard, calling himself Young, had cornered Jamal near the bookstall. His works had been acquired by museums in New York and Delhi and Frankfurt. Now he wanted to make an impression in Ontario, and he was appealing to Jamal as a community leader and lawyer. He showed Jamal some photographs of his works, designs for fountains and monuments containing whorls and mazes, abstract figures human and animal, phalluses. Jamal, trapped, could only muster, "Wow! You made these?"

Young took back his photographs. "Commissions!" he said sharply, slapping his hand with the bundle.

"You mean you can make them – "

"If you get me the commissions."

"Ah, my friend, in a few years – "

"In a few years I'll be dead. I'm suffering from a terminal disease." He walked away, disappointed.

At Sixty-nine, however, over the coming months a completely new and unschooled artistic career began. One of the numerous anonymous gifts Esmail had received was a supply of art materials. His legs continued to ache, especially in the cold, and he was, essentially, disabled. So Esmail started to paint. From what hidden resources, what buried memory, this passion drew its energy, even he could not have said. But passion it was. The first report of his work arrived when a social worker who came to see him saw the paintings. One newspaper printed a photo of the artist surrounded by his works. It said that he had an apocalyptic vision and a gift for colour.

This was a lot of hype, as Nanji reported to Jamal. "Esmail belongs to no school or tradition. He paints garishly, that's his so-called gift for colour. And he paints these meek people praying . . . both his gift for colour and apocalyptic vision you can buy for a few dollars at any gift store at Bloor and Dufferin. They are patronizing him."

An art critic from the *Globe and Mail* came to look at Esmail's work, and hastily departed. An editor from a literary magazine, who had been present at the protest rally, came. He talked for a long time with Esmail, but took no notes and lost interest after looking at a few pictures.

But Esmail persisted, doggedly. He took art lessons, with Nanji's encouragement, at the Art Gallery of Ontario. But the lessons, to Nanji's disappointment, seemed hardly to affect the way he painted. He would go to class and do his thing – the instructor left him alone. At most, it seemed, he acquired a facility for the use of equipment. Yet he painted as if there were no tomorrow. He even painted the walls of his bedroom, which his sister would open for exhibit when he was not around. Two of his larger works were duly hung in the lobby of Sixty-nine. Then one morning, approximately a year after the attack on him, he announced to the A-T gathering at the foot of the goddess, "I am going to Dar."

There was silence. Then someone spoke.

"For what?"

"Holiday." There was a wide grin on his face, a rare event in any circumstance.

"How long?"

"I don't know."

"You're crazy. Go to Florida."

Esmail went to Dar, and never came back. His sister, who stayed on in Toronto, maintained he was still a Canadian citizen.

If there was anything Jamal learned from the Don Mills demo, it was that the world was a bigger place, and he had to grab it, make a prominent place for himself in it. The two-dimensional world of Sixty-nine and its neighbours was a dead one, a world to escape from. Accordingly, he took his chance when it eventually came.

First he married a "good" girl: respectable and educated, practical and with both feet planted firmly on the ground as only a Dar girl could be, with whom he could talk – as he told Nanji – as only with a Dar girl. But she was English. Young and average-looking, tending to plumpness. She worked at a bookstore downtown. Jamal had met her at the demo and dated her for several months. She was not taken in by Jamal's bluster, Nanji could see, but she was affectionate. The wedding reception the following June was grand, so it could be seen as one not to be easily forgotten, a rite of passage to which prominent people of all races were invited; in which a Dar friend, a former socialist and Hyde Park orator turned men's haberdasher, introduced the bride and groom in a speech delivered in British accent and with much aplomb (in which Jamal himself did not miss the chance to say a few humorous though not tasteless words). After the wedding he took his bride to Halifax, Nova Scotia, to get a Canadian law degree for his eventual admission to the Ontario Bar.

At Sixty-nine he was missed. His raucous, cackling laughter, his sense of humour, the disconcerting directness, his presence among Dar's unemployed at the A-T in the mornings, his flirting with the young girls, and his lecherous look. Nanji watched him go with a sense of envy eating deep inside him. Jamal was going into the world to conquer it, and conquer it he would if he played his cards right and did not fall. For himself, Nanji felt, with a certain foreboding, that his life had been lived, he had seen, done, felt so much in his own small but intense ways. But he was yet to be stung and brought alive again.

10

Three years had passed since that blustery winter night when the Lalanis stood outside the Toronto airport, contemplating a mode of transportation. Much had happened in that period and there was, in a sense, no looking back. The children were well on their way, "Canadians" now, or almost. There were many new faces in the buildings of Rosecliffe Park, and many others had disappeared, to Mississauga, Scarborough, and even as far away as Calgary. There were a few stories of success now, one of them about Jamal, who had returned and was practising as a lawyer. For many others, Nurdin among them, life simply "went along."

And then one warm Saturday night, near the plaster goddess in the lobby of Sixty-nine, Nurdin Lalani had a bizarre encounter: an encounter which set in motion a chain of events that would relentlessly take him in directions he had not thought of, open up a world for which he was not quite prepared.

He had returned from the corner store with milk for the next day. Only one elevator was working, and someone was not letting it go. Perhaps because of the day's traffic, on weekend evenings the air inside the lobby feels spent and lifeless, oppressive almost, you want badly to get away. He was getting tired watching the lighted panel. The elevator was on twelve and would not budge. Should he walk up? No.

He turned around at a sound. The goddess of the building was sending forth a man. A short young man.

"You Indian, man?" he said to Nurdin.

He didn't know what to answer. India or Pakistan, what difference? What struck him about this man was his dark face and the bright orange jacket he wore.

"I am from East Africa," Nurdin said finally.

"I been watching for Indian face, man. You is the first. I am Mohan. I am from Guyana."

Nurdin was at a loss for words. He looked at the man and smiled. He had heard of Guyana, had never met anyone from there. He had been told they had names like Mike Singh and John Shamsudeen. What do I say to him? he wondered.

"Are there many Indians in Guyana?" Where *was* Guyana – somewhere near Ghana or Guinea?

Another shuffle and from behind the goddess another such person, a woman from the same place, Nurdin guessed.

"She is my wife, Lakshmi."

Nurdin smiled. Lakshmi, really – wasn't *that* what they called the plaster goddess herself?

"She carrying baby in her belly." Mohan cupped a hand on his wife's belly, to indicate. She wore a black skirt and a white blouse that needed tucking in. She didn't say a word, just stood there looking down, as if in shame.

"She tired, bhai. You Indian, you understand."

"She needs rest. You should take her home. It's too late for her."

"But that be the trouble, bhai. The car is broke down, bhai. Is why we stranded – not knowing nobody and nothing 'round here."

"Where is it?"

"Outside."

"Call a taxi. Pick up your car tomorrow."

The man was silent. Obviously they didn't have the money.

"Where do you live?" Nurdin asked.

"Brampton. With my brother. You see me and Lakshmi, we is visiting from Guyana."

"You are visiting! Let's call your brother."

"He visiting in Montreal. Is coming back late tonight."

The elevator came. No wonder it was stuck on twelve, someone was moving out of the building.

"Please. You Indian, you understand."

"What-what?"

"We'll just sit. Lakshmi here will sit. Until the morning, bhai. We've nowhere to go."

Lakshmi, Nurdin realized, had been crying. That's what she'd been doing behind the goddess. Now she was crying again. God, she was tired, he could see that. Mohan put his hand on her belly for effect. Only for her, Nurdin thought. The man – a boy, really – didn't impress him. Only for her sake, he would agree.

"Let's go," Nurdin said. And wondered what Zera and the kids would say.

Zera, seeing them enter, simply smiled, the gracious hostess welcoming her husband's friends. "Sit, sit," Nurdin said. They sat on the couch, Mohan lying back, his feet just touching the carpet; Lakshmi, nervous, watched Zera with apprehension. Zera stood there with a fixed smile.

"So this is our humble abode," said Nurdin, himself sitting on a chair across from them.

Zera finally spoke. "You'll have tea?" she said to the girl. The girl nodded eagerly, and Zera disappeared into the kitchen.

"The washroom is there," said Nurdin, pointing, then, after a brief pause, he got up as if he'd suddenly remembered something and went to the kitchen.

"Their car broke down. The girl was crying, she's tired."

"Have they called someone?"

He explained. There was nothing they could do but let them stay the night.

They all had tea and chatted. Lakshmi not only found her tongue, she could talk as much and more intelligently than her husband. The host and hostess were impressed. Sometimes Mohan would abruptly cut her short with a contradiction, and she would quiet down for a little sulk while he went on, then she would join in again.

For sleeping arrangements, they let the couple have the living room, Lakshmi the couch and Mohan the floor.

"I prefer the floor anytime, man. The floor good for the back, like I always say."

With that, they left them. Hanif and Fatima had been told in a hurried conference and had gone away, grumbling, to bed.

Once in their room, behind the closed door, sitting on the bed, Nurdin and Zera realized the situation they were in – a strange couple inside the apartment with them. They could be faking. Even the girl. Suppose, one chance in a million, they were faking. All the incidents one hears of, reads about, the gruesome crimes. A strange couple in the living room between the two bedrooms, between them and their children. Even if the girl was genuine – she had to be – the man was definitely a no-good. His breath. He'd definitely been drinking. And the way he cut her short, right there, in front of Nurdin and Zera, their hosts, unable to control himself. There had been a lie she caught him in, quite innocently it seemed, for which she earned a scowl. And that mark on her mouth, a small dark scar, you would hardly notice, unless it was pointed out. And *he* pointed it out: "She hit herself on the sewing machine." Who cared, such a small insignificant remark – unless, of course, he beat her. No wonder she'd been crying. "Another Abdul," said Nurdin to a quiet Zera.

Even if he was a drinking wife-beater and nothing else, they decided they couldn't take chances. They would take turns sleeping, one of them keeping watch, giving ear to the snores already coming from the living room. But sleep overcame this resolve, and they woke up with the sun shining on their faces and the kids shaking them.

Lakshmi and Mohan too had to be woken up, and they got up in a daze, having dreamed perhaps of Guyana, seeing four strange faces in a strange room. Everyone was in good spirits, the fears of the night swept away by the brilliant, cheerful glare coming through the window and the balcony doors. Zera went to make puris, and Mohan telephoned his brother and gave him the address.

Romesh, the brother, was taller than Mohan, with a short-cropped beard that had turned white. But he seemed to be about the same age as Nurdin. He walked in, in sandals and bush shirt, with a little grin on his face.

"Man," he said to Nurdin, "I admire you. To take this couple in without even knowing them!"

"What could we do?" But never again, said Nurdin to himself.

"He's my brother, but he's a bum, I don't mind telling you – "

"My brother Romesh. He always the one for joke and laughter."

"What do you do in Toronto, Nurdin? You running a shop or something?" Romesh had eyes that never rested. Even the paint on the wall came under scrutiny. The plastic chandelier, gathering dust. The photograph on the wall. The Masai woodcarving. The wax Taj Mahal. Nurdin waited until the eyes stopped moving, and Romesh continued, "Eh, Nurdin? What do you do?"

Nurdin explained the series of jobs that had come to nothing.

"If you are looking for something, I know just the thing for you."

"The goddess was testing us, eh?" He grinned at Zera later. Good deeds are rewarded. Didn't the gods assume human forms in order to test mortals? Obviously they had passed the test, for he got the job at the Ontario Addiction Centre. General purpose attendant, pushing trolleys of linen or tea, sorting and delivering mail. They would have made him wear khaki, in Dar, for such a job. Errand boy – but never mind. The pay was not bad. There were two coffee breaks and one free meal at the cafeteria. The benefits were good. The doctors were not going to load his aging back with crates. And for his bosom buddy at work, he had none other than the suave Romesh.

Not long after, that summer, Nanji's girlfriend, as the Lalanis called her in spite of his objections, finally came to Toronto for a visit, with two other friends, and Nanji's life also took a new turn.

Days before, because Nanji had announced to the Lalanis, the whole of Sixty-nine Rosecliffe seemed abuzz with the news of their arrival. Nanji's prestige rose – three girls coming to see him from America, there must be something to him. He didn't show anything of course, not externally, but you could see there was something beneath that calm surface, straining under the excitement, the pressure of a large happiness.

Before they arrived, he had gone looking for supplies: pillows, sleeping bags, blankets, cups, plates – what it takes to convert two rooms into a home. The word passed at Sixty-nine, and feeling the curious, amused, kindly eyes on him in the corridors as he passed with whatever else it was he needed, he would blush.

He wouldn't have to worry about food, there were enough volunteers for the good cause: he just had to give a few hours' notice. Zera went to help him clean his quarters. Nurdin went along to give the final word, but actually to see the apartment. The Lalanis had never been invited before, and they could see why. There was a bed, a TV, which Fatima and Hanif quickly discovered wasn't working, an armchair. And books. An attempt had been made to shelve them, but they had long since overrun the solitary shelf and were pouring out of it, in a trail that bypassed the two heaps on either side of the armchair and ended in another heap at the bed. There was no rug on the floor and there were posters on the wall, with sayings and pictures of people they didn't recognize.

Nurdin went and sat down on the green padded armchair. A handsome, comfortable thing, wearing the dull gloss of long use. He sank into it and leaned back. "So, you sit in this chair, and the three girls on your lap." Even Fatima and Hanif couldn't help laughing.

"I assure you I can do better, I just haven't got around to it."

"*When* will you get around to it then?"

"Nurdin," implored Zera, "go with him and find something, please. Unwanted furniture – Ramju has a table – and look for a rug. Ask the superintendent. Look at the For Sale signs. Go now."

And magically, in two days, two hours before the girls came, a pleasant apartment was there to greet them. Some of it had been repainted. Even the windowpanes had been cleaned. Nanji had taken the opportunity to get a new bed, buy bright things for the walls, furnish the kitchen. Everything else was on loan, indefinitely.

And when they came, what happy faces, what life they brought with them, what exuberance! It was, apparently, a long-awaited reunion, not only for Nanji but also for the girls, who had come from different cities. The squeals of joy they gave on seeing him, the hugging in the open. Nurdin had been with Nanji when the girls arrived, in a taxi, and had witnessed somewhat embarrassedly their easy manner. How you wish you were young again, oh how you'd like to start afresh. Nanji was puffed up like a peacock. And why not. Three girls had come just to be with him in his apartment. They wined and dined – of the wine Nurdin was certain though he did not tell Zera. They went out, they came late and stayed up practically all night consuming samosas and kebabs, chatting and laughing, shouting and squealing. Three days and nights of living free, and then they left on Sunday afternoon. And on that depressing Sunday Nanji came to them, broken.

Before Yasmin left, she had given the message she had come to give: she was marrying. What do you tell a young man whose heart is broken – there will be others? There is no pleasure without pain? "But you said there was nothing," Zera had said. "Nothing definite, but she always gave hope. . . . " "If there was nothing, she wouldn't come here to tell him, would she," explained Nurdin to Zera, a little too wisely.

Nanji was loath to return to his apartment, to those rooms now empty, echoing already in such a short time, with memories, and sat up late with the Lalanis. They wanted to retire, but they waited patiently, plying him with hot tea to soothe his pain. Finally he went.

He continued to come, almost every day for a couple of weeks, to talk, be comforted, to be told that she was not worth having, she who had done this to him. "I will find you a nice girl," Zera told him. She did show him a few, but he simply shook his head, smiling to show he appreciated the gesture.

Then he stopped coming, embarrassed at having clung to them, having revealed so much to them, such tender spots, and they understood. Once or twice they had had fun at his expense; he had not been amused, they quickly realized. Fatima and Hanif, going their own way with baseball and hockey and their own friends, also had less time for him. Nanji's worth in their eyes had dipped a little, but they still held him in awe to an extent he was not aware of and were relieved he disappeared so they could think of him as his old self.

For Nurdin Lalani a new life had begun with his job at the Ontario Addiction Centre. With it he had accepted a station in life – not one he believed he deserved, a son of a prominent elder and businessman, but one which would have to do. At least he could say, in mosque and at Sixty-nine, that he had a job downtown. He didn't have to say precisely what job. "Say manager," Zera told him. "You do manage supply rooms."

Romesh's companionship made the work more tolerable, sometimes even enjoyable, although he had had to get used to the man. Romesh had a way of edging into his confidence, assuming a familiarity, that had startled him at first. That, and his different idiom and accent.

One day they were having their lunch together. Nurdin noticed something on Romesh's plate and asked, "Is that a hot dog?"

How could he not have known. Surely that was Satan speaking through him. Romesh cut it in two, neatly, and gave him half. "Like hot dog, but better. Try it."

He ate a piece and it was good. Even before he had finished swallowing it, as it was going down his gullet, everything inside him was echoing the after-taste, crying, "Foreign, foreign." Yet it did nothing to him.

When Romesh returned with a second helping, he had finished his half. Romesh nodded approvingly. "That was sausage."

"Beef, I hope."

"No."

He pretended shock, and Romesh comforted him. "See, you're the same. Nothing's happened to you. Forget pork, man, I was not supposed to eat *meat*. Even egg. I'm supposed to think you're dirty. You think *they* are dirty. Who is right? Superstitions, all."

The pig, they said, was the most beastly of beasts. It ate garbage and faeces, even its babies, it copulated freely, was incestuous. Wallowed in muck. Eat pig and become a beast. Slowly the bestial traits – cruelty and promiscuity, in one word, godlessness – overcame you. And you became, morally, like *them*. The Canadians.

There were those, claiming to be scientific, who said it's the diseases the pig carries and the quality of meat, which has long-term effects, which are the reason for the prohibition: the Book has all knowledge for all time. And there was Nanji – who himself drank wine, Nurdin knew, and probably ate pork – who said it's the discipline that's important, you've been forbidden to do it for whatever reason, and that's that.

In any case, he, Nurdin, had eaten *it* – he could not make himself name "it" yet – and perhaps that is where the real rot began, inside him.

It was amusing to Nanji, Nurdin's concern about the effects of pork-eating. It was so obvious he'd tasted pork and was groping for an argument to absolve himself. Zera of course had supplied the standard line, pseudoscience: "Eat pig and become a pig." But Nurdin had sought an answer from him, Nanji the educated, and Nanji had told the simple truth: eating pork was forbidden by the faith, by God, reasons did not matter. Nurdin had opened his mouth, almost retorted, Have you had pork? But had shut it again, why? Perhaps afraid, he, Nanji, would have asked him the same thing. Then Nurdin asked, "But can it change you, from inside, you know, your character?" He'd been kind and said simply, "No."

Of course, it depends on what you mean by "change you." Molecules are the same whether they are in beef or pork, or even in yourself. If pork has chemicals that alter your mental state, you could find those chemicals elsewhere too. So why pork? No. It is *you* who have changed when you attempt, even think about, eating pork the first time. And once you've had it, the first time, tasted that taste so distinct you cannot cheat yourself, you are no longer the same man: something has turned inside you, with a definite click. Unless you go into an orgy of remorse and repentance – and who does, these days? – and perhaps even then you cannot regain what you've lost.

So, Nurdin has changed.

They had come to watch the Canada Day fireworks. Parked the car half a mile away and trudged along with the crowd, to the lakeshore, all at Fatima's insistence. This was the thing to do, act like Canadians, for chrissakes! All this playing cards and chatting and discussing silly topics while glugging tea by the gallon and eating samosas – is not Canadian. Not realizing that most of the Canadians she knew and met were like her, with parents not too different from hers. So, while others of their building celebrated at the eighteenth floor open house, watching fireworks from a distance and perhaps getting a better view of them – and, yes, with tea and samosas, and gossip, and men teasing the women – the Lalanis with Nanji had come to where the action was. Had eaten those fat, luscious french fries and assiduously avoided – Nanji couldn't help catching Nurdin's eye – the hot dogs for sale on the sidewalks.

He could remember other fireworks, on Fourths of July, in New York. The two of them, he and "she," with a blanket to sit on, a picnic basket with beer, with books to read, waiting patiently for the fireworks. So "with it." Even then he'd not been too impressed with such displays. He always saw them beforehand, in his mind, exploding into brilliant colours, and not only that, the sparks forming precise patterns and shapes suspended in the atmosphere before fading away. Flags – the Stars and Stripes, the Maple Leaf – rockets, whatever. Instead, they turned out so ordinary. You oohed and aahed at something slightly less mediocre than the previous. But it wasn't the fireworks he had gone for, he had gone for her. To be with her, his composite "she," the nemesis, Yasmin.

Across the lake now on the island was another crowd, no less – or more – enthusiastic than they were. The lights were sparser there, as was the crowd, and a large blackness hung behind them. Nanji stared hard at the points of light in the blackness until his eyes watered. Something, not inside, had turned for him, also with a definite click. A phase of life had ended, or would soon end – the warning had been given.

The girls' visit had been fun. Yasmin, characteristically, had come with piles of tourist literature, the itinerary planned. More or less. Of course she overdid it, would get tired – the first one to do so – and suggest, having made up her mind in any case: "How about calling it quits here." That love of life and that weakness. You adored her for that, felt tenderness for her, and she needed that. The day trip to Montreal had failed to materialize simply because the previous night had been too short. And because, so far, there had been too much eating and drinking, a jog through the park was suggested with a sorrowful slap at a belly not quite yet flabby. There followed for Nanji one of his most embarrassing moments, walking through the corridor and then going down in the crowded elevator, a giraffe in bright new shorts in the company of three loud girls in designer track suits. In the pathway he'd looked up to see – just in case – and his fears were confirmed: there were spectators on the balconies.

A large get-together had always been planned for 1984 – a significant reunion in a significant year, that might yet come but looked difficult to pull off. This small one was her accomplishment – *their* accomplishment, to give due credit to the other two girls. A kindness, as he later realized, to him.

They had been, originally, a group of six, of roughly the same age, from roughly the same place. A prominent East African group of emigrés, former students meeting in Boston and New York and Washington, for Thanksgiving and Fourth of July and Christmas, and because of their mobility they were well known to the new groups of immigrants and refugees shakily setting themselves up. They were the Second Original Group, they always pointed out, the first one having come eight years before on extravagant African-American programs, having got married, all of them well settled and gone to ground.

A fate which had already befallen two of the guys in their own group. It was always understood that the friendships were too close for anything else to come out of them: except for he and "she," a subject rarely mentioned, and then only among the guys and, for all he knew, the girls. Anyway, Salim and Karim had married two nice and proper girls, from Canada, and had, effectively, disappeared. Which left Nanji and the three girls. There was Shamim, with those classical Indian features, perpetually caught in a soft light, as it were, all curves and not a sharp corner. The small chin, the long eyelashes, and dark black eyes, the beautiful puckered smile. All waiting for Mr. Perfect. And Dilu, with curly hair, a sharp mind, and an equally sharp tongue. Rather attractive, though her dark tones gave a first impression – but only first – that did not do her justice. Also waiting for Mr. Perfect. And Yasmin, with numerous friends and acquaintances from all corners of the world, had not met her idea of perfection either.

On the last day of the visit they had decided to go to the lakeshore and take a ferry to the islands. After morning coffee at the Hilton, Dilu and Shamim decided to walk to Harbourfront and the antique market, leaving Nanji and Yasmin alone to go to the island, find a spot, and await the two sightseers.

It was bliss to be together with her after God knows how long. The day was gorgeous. They crossed to Hanlan's Point in the company of an army of cyclists. From there they took a round trip on a little train to Centre Island. She couldn't resist, just as she couldn't resist those horse-drawn carriages in New York at Christmas. Could he ever have so much fun alone, or with anyone else?

Then they walked, found a quiet place to sit. Small planes were taking off in the distance, another one droned overhead pulling a sign. Men and women playing soccer, a toddler taking his first steps running after a balloon, a single man with book and picnic basket, french bread and all.

She looked so beautiful – not the beauty of perfection but of life. The ponytail he had known many years ago, in schooldays when he didn't even talk to her, was gone, of course, the hair was contemporary-short. There were a few freckles on the face. Her eyes when not twinkling were fiery, her mouth was generous and could produce delicious chuckles. She was fairly tall, did not look dwarfed beside him as many Dar girls did. Yet there was this frailty in her. She could be easily broken, as he told himself so many times. . . .

You chew on a shoot of grass watching her, then you realize it's not good for you. You cast it aside and immediately pull out another one. . . . Your heart is full, you swallow, you know she feels your gaze on her and must look up. She does.

"You know the first time you came to New York . . . " she said.

"Yes?"

"I've never gotten over it – insisting on coming up. I thought, Another fresh guy, him I can handle, and then at the door solemnly turning about!"

133

"Funny, wasn't it. But I knew what you were thinking. I wanted to prove you wrong."

"You did. That was thoughtful of you, going out of your way. I could have taken a cab – I do that every day."

"I couldn't help it. I can't help it – feeling concerned." He paused, a long pause. "I care for you."

Had alarm bells rung, had he grabbed the opportunity, sensing this was the last moment.

"I know," she said. "You must have wondered why I never wrote or called you back. I must have sounded rather abrupt when you called that time."

"You did."

She actually sighed.

"I've gone through a lot these past months. It's almost been a year. You see, when you called, there was someone else."

It was done, delivered, as gently as possible. And he was felled.

"Who?"

"He's an Arab – Egyptian."

"What does he do? A banker?"

She laughed. "You always thought I was looking for a banker to marry."

"Or an ambassador."

"He works at the United Nations. Actually, he's very gentle – like you."

"Then what was wrong with me?"

"You don't know how hard it's been for me. And for him. You see, I told him about you. And his mother – she's against it."

Then they had taken the ferry back. The two others had not arrived. It had all been conveniently arranged, this assassination at a quiet spot. How could you blame her though, we do what we have to do. He was completely recovered, to look at, when finally the two other girls came. Did he only imagine those sidelong glances searching for visible wounds?

To lose such good friends. Dilu and Shamim – when would he see them again, would it ever be the same again? When they left in a cab, all shouting, "1984!" and yelling at the driver, "Don't worry, we'll pay the fine, go, go!" the only place he could go to fill the emptiness inside him was the Lalanis'.

He was grateful to the Lalanis, even for the dreadful copies of herself that Zera introduced him to. He realized perhaps he had come too close, and kept much to himself after that. Until today, when the kids needed his company at the fireworks. They walked back to the car with the feeling somehow that the excitement was yet to come. He took them to a falafel place on Bloor Street. The kids loved it; he rose once more in their esteem. The parents saw no big deal to it. It was all bhajia and chappati, cooked differently, that's all.

11

Ever since that first act of serious incontinence – tasting a bit of pork sausage and then proceeding to consume a sizeable chunk of it – Nurdin's sins, it seemed to him, had multiplied. Thinking back on a statement Nanji had made, he could find some explanation for his predicaments and even a little comfort for his inner turmoils. Nanji, he said to himself, had hit the nail right on the head! Well, they didn't give out degrees for nothing. You've got to have something up here. You are *already* changed when you think about eating pork. Think about *that*. There must be something in the Canadian air that changes

136

us, as the old people say. The old people who are shunted between sons and daughters and old peoples' homes – who would have thought that possible only a few years ago. It's all in the air: the divorces, crimes you could never have imagined before, children despising their parents. An image of his own arrogant Fatima came to his mind and he pushed it back.

There was this nice young couple at number Seventy-one: respectable, pious. They had met in mosque doing voluntary service, married, and were expecting their first child. What could be more gratifying to watch and reflect upon: the couple strolling back from mosque, parents of a new generation. Then baby was born, but it had blue eyes. It took some doing by the young man's family before he would believe what his own eyes told him, and the wife confessed to the truth. The couple were divorced now, and the girl was living with the father of the baby. What is more, it had all been accepted as the way the world is. What was once unthinkable became acceptable. Roshan, Zera's sister, continued to be battered at home. Already in the last few months twice she had come with puffed-up face to spend the night. Nurdin was all for calling the police: "Let them lock up the pig" (yes, pig, he had said). But the women said no, hush-hush, don't wash your dirty linen in public. Well, hadn't they heard, that is precisely what you do, there are laundromats here. This is Canada, he told Roshan, giving back her own. She had returned home the following day, after being nursed by Zera, as for the next round at boxing. Wait till her son grows older, two or three years from now, he'll beat the shit out of his father. . . .

He looked at Zera. No carnal sin from *that* quarter, he thought, eyeing the ample hips move under her favourite sack dress as she dusted the table. She was in the greatest of spirits because, after long entreaties, several years of pleading, the Master, Missionary himself, had decided to come and settle in Canada. The arrival was several months away, the dusting and vacuuming today was only to make the place look like it should for the Master. Nurdin was pleading earache and resting on his favourite chair. And looking at Zera.

Even though she had grown fat, there *was* still an attraction about her. There was that friendliness, the soft-heartedness, and the sense of humour. Those breasts were still ripe mangoes and the large hips were yet firm. But she did not let him come close. Blocking his attentions, in bed, turning against his desires that mountain of a haunch, behind which he felt rather helpless and small. Do you want me to come from behind? If you want to. With this Kilimanjaro facing me? Go to sleep.

Zera was married to God, the idea of God. Not that she was otherworldly or excessively devotional. Her obsession was to discuss God and religion, and she liked nothing better than to sit at the feet of her teacher, Missionary, and to hear him discourse on God, the Prophet, the sages. A little like listening to expert commentary on sports. If there was any devotion, it was to the Master. There had been in the past, on one or two occasions, innuendoes at this unhealthy worship of Missionary by his female followers. Nurdin knew his wife, not to say Missionary, and was never bothered. And, after all – thinking back on those innuendoes – who could know the innermost secrets of the heart, even if they were your wife's . . . or husband's . . . or your own. . . .

They had not been physically really close for years. Not had sex – what a nice legitimate way of putting it. He had resigned himself to this celibacy. There was so much to do, to worry about. And now this late reawakening, a blossoming in middle age of a youthful obsession. Will it pass? He shuddered, felt the almost physical impact from the steely eyes he knew were staring at him from the picture on the wall – should I let it pass?

Romesh had observed it. Romesh with the roving eye had observed his roving eye, and his shyness with women.

"That big wife of yours not letting you have it?"

It rather shocked Nurdin at first, this open remark about his wife. "She is very pious, very religious, you know."

Romesh had a simple solution, an idea Nurdin was not quite ignorant about, especially in his youth. So he tried just taking her one night, but she had given such a scream, a yelp, that Fatima and Hanif came running, Fatima lumbering in the lead. Zera did not help him with explanations, she let him go to sleep with the knowledge that the kids already guessed what had happened.

To be young in this land free of inhibitions. What did he care of morality, can you change the way the world is going? He regretted his innocent youth somewhat. Once, when he was a boy, the picture of a beauty-contest winner had been printed in the newspaper, a white girl in a swimsuit, and they had all looked at it gravely in his home, at dinner, his father first. The picture had gone round the table. Then Nurdin had secretly cut it out and hid it among the pages of his exercise book. Later someone had removed it, he didn't know who, presumably to protect him from his father's wrath. In place of the picture of Angela (that was the girl's name), there was the traditional peacock feather. That was the extent to which he had let his desire run away, more or less, barring moments in the bathroom. He wished sometimes he had gone fornicating with the boys in the alleys and byways, in the huts with Arab and African prostitutes. Or in the quarters where Indian women ran the same trade more furtively and at higher price. He had even accompanied his friends on such expeditions. All, or most, respectable men now. Like Jamal, who had done everything in his youth. Now he was respectable and rich. Then there was that Nanji. Difficult to make out what Nanji was. A Sufi, you would think, an ascetic. But he had spent three days – and, worse, nights – with three women, drinking and doing God knows what. Zera had not really approved, of course, in spite of her enthusiasm in fixing up Nanji's apartment, though she had blamed not Nanji but the three girls. Pretty girls, all. Pretty and free.

Nurdin's lusty eye, he had discovered, hovered not only on the ample but forbidden body of his wife – which God would surely excuse – but on practically all women, it seemed. Like a boy at puberty he had become aware of Woman, the female of the species, and he found her diverse and beautiful. And what was offered to an eye starved for such visions was simply breathtaking. It was like sending to the hungry of the world not just rations of wheat but whole banquets. Bra-less women with lively breasts under blouses and T-shirts that simply sucked your eyeballs out. Buttocks breaking out of shorts. And when you saw these twin delights nuzzling a bicycle seat, doing a gentle rhythmic dance of their own in the dazzling heat and among the trees and flowers and the smells of nature in the park – why, you had to be sure you were dressed right. And Zera marching along ahead. "Hurry up, Nurdin, stop loitering like a boy." Boy, indeed. His head would be pounding, his body aching with desire.

Later, after witnessing such a vision, he would be overcome by bouts of guilt. The picture on the wall fixing him with its eyes, reminding him of that hymn, "Lust and anger, those two you shall avoid." Anger was not his problem, that was his father's. Let *him* pay for it. Nurdin's problem was lust. Don't covet another man's woman. Well, what if yours doesn't give? The punishment for backbiting was to be hung by your tongue, and for listening to back-bite, to be hung by your ears. And for fornicating? A gruesome image of himself hanging by his balls intruded into his mind. He stifled a giggle. He didn't remember who had listed those punishments, probably one of his father's cronies during their interminable sessions. Hell will have scorpions as large as camels. And the sinful will cry in anguish, mercy, mercy.

One day Romesh and he had got out early from work, a little after lunch. It was election day. They stood outside, hands in their pockets, looking, feeling, small next to the impressive broad building from which they had emerged.

"Well, what do you intend to do for the rest of the afternoon," Romesh said.

"Go home, I think." The bus stop was a block away on Spadina.

"Tell you what, Nur. Let's go for a walk."

"Here?" A casual, aimless walk in the streets was not something he had done for a long time.

"Let's go to Yonge Street."

"Yeah, let's go to Yonge Street." He liked driving on it on Friday nights with the family, to see the gaiety and lights, and hear the noisy crowds on the streets and music at each corner. Pretending not to see the prostitutes in tight skirts and heavy makeup.

He had walked on Yonge Street perhaps once. He could now see why. The daytime crowd made walking difficult. The street was littered and congested with noisy traffic, many of the shops were dingy if not outright disreputable. There was nothing much to see.

They sat down at a rather fashionable-looking outdoor café. "This is the life, man," said Romesh with a sigh. "I could sit here forever, just watching the people go by."

"And life go by, eh?" Sometimes he never knew how to talk to this man.

"And life go by, alas."

The waitress was young and pretty, attentive. "Well, what can I do for you gentlemen today."

"Plenty. But for now. . . . " Romesh said with a grin.

Nurdin had a coffee, Romesh a beer. They sat and watched in silence. At work there was enough to talk about, they saw each other all the time, had lunch in the cafeteria together.

"Hey, would you like to taste my beer?"

"Oh, no."

"There is nothing wrong with tasting, you know. From what I know of the Quran, only getting intoxicated is forbidden."

Nurdin knew the argument. It was the latest among the educated Dar crowd before they too relented.

"You could have three or four beers easily without getting drunk."

That Nurdin had also heard. "Let me try a sip." His coffee cup was empty, in any case. He concentrated his mind on drinking that sip, so that it would not wander off and summon guilt from somewhere. That accomplished, he sat back and watched Romesh finish the drink. Finally he had a glass of his own, to accompany Romesh's second. He did not know why he was doing what he was doing, did not think about it, though a vague consciousness of his deed lay somewhat heavily on his heart. The beer was refreshing, the bitter taste he got used to. His eyes were soon glazing over, he only hoped that no one walking by on Yonge Street would recognize him. They were sitting at a most conspicuous spot. The beer mug before him could not be mistaken for anything else.

"There's nothing to see on Yonge Street, eh?" he said.

"Ah, if you want to really see something. . . . " Romesh grinned. "Let's corrupt you some more." They got up.

They walked two blocks south to a part of the street where the pedestrian traffic thinned. They stood outside a place called Dar es Salaam, The Heaven of Love. It was a name you couldn't miss – not if you came from a place called Dar es Salaam. The name of this heaven was printed on an oriental-style red canopy with a nude drawing to highlight it.

"Where do you say you come from, eh, Nur? This should feel quite like home to you."

"What is it?"

"Follow me."

Romesh went in, he followed. What promised opulence from outside turned out to be, inside, a narrow corridor: unswept, oil-painted yellow walls now grimy. On the walls some framed photos of nude girls, pubic hair conspicuous. There was a window just inside the entrance, from which Romesh got some change and counted half of it into Nurdin's hand. "Enjoy. It's all on me, man. All on me."

There were six booths inside, two of them taken, each with a pair of viewers – like binoculars – to see through. You put a quarter into a slot – no, first you put your eyes on the viewer, instinctively, then you looked for the slot and put a quarter there, and you leaned forward on the viewer and pressed home the coin.

Nurdin's heart pounded violently against a chest that seemed to have contracted. He had never seen anything like it, not in ads, not in movies, nor even the girlie magazines of his youth. Sex scenes beyond his wildest dreams: dirty, depraved, exciting – how *much* the flesh was capable of! It was enough to destabilize you forever, question all the inhibitions and prohibitions of childhood and youth – do this, don't do that: who had thought them up? Reluctantly he looked up from the viewer, worked up to quite a state. He had used up all his coins.

As they were walking out two very young prostitutes in tight leather miniskirts stood around, vigorously chewing gum. "How about the real thing now, boys?" said one.

"Sorry. We are booked, ladies," grinned Romesh.

"Fags."

"Now to go home for the fun, eh, Nur. Why pay when you can get it free. Your big woman obliges now, I hope? My trick worked, I bet. What did I tell you. They *like* it."

He went home oppressed with guilt. "What's the matter, Nurdin?" Zera asked. "Oh, a headache." He kept well away from her, his eyes averted, two cardamom pods in his mouth to sweeten his breath. To punish himself, he looked full square at Haji Lalani's photograph, eye to eye. Do to me what you will: twenty-five, fifty, a hundred strokes of hippo-hide whip, dipped in salt. When he died, his father would be waiting for him with the whip, God's personal executioner. . . .

They had gone to Montreal one weekend, in the car. All outings were prescribed by Fatima: "We don't *go* anywhere." Her outings with her friends were still strictly controlled by her mother, though she was beginning to break away. So to Montreal it was, on a long weekend, where they stayed at a motel owned by a family they had known in Dar. After doing the usual round of sightseeing, on the last day they had tea with Nurdin's niece, the daughter of his elder brother, Akber, who had gone on to Belgian Congo, been looted a couple of times in the civil wars there, and had finally settled in Belgium. Only the most rudimentary correspondence had been maintained with him – marriages, deaths – and this latest from him: that his daughter was in Montreal with her husband and children. Naturally they were all excited at the prospect of meeting a European niece and cousin they had never seen.

The house was on an expensive-looking street, and in it they met the most graceful people, the kind in the old days you would have called "civilized." His niece Nermine was tall and simply beautiful, in a long white dress, her hair braided and fashioned stylishly in what Nurdin was pretty certain was an African style: thin braids raised above the head, revealing a long elegant neck. Watching her your heart missed a beat. She spoke French, Dutch, and English, and a little very accented Gujarati. The two children, boys, spoke English with a most delightful French accent. The husband was quiet, attentive, in a red polo-neck sweater and immaculately pressed trousers. There was even a dog, who was locked away. The table they sat at, of solid wood, was covered in a spotless white cloth. On it were plates and silverware, some of which they didn't know how to handle. The tea cups clinked brightly, calling attention. They all talked pleasantries, most of their attention taken in doing the right thing at the table. One thing he found out: his brother Akber had a diamond-cutting business in a town called Antwerp.

It was a depressing visit. They had come out of the house as grim as if leaving a funeral. Nurdin felt as he would have when walking out of the headmaster's office with a sore bottom recently whipped, with an unpleasant experience never mentioned, best forgotten. Not that it was his niece's fault. She was polite enough. But they had felt so out of place, *he* had felt like a bum, with his night watchman's blue jacket, unpressed trousers, cheap boots straight out of Honest Ed's. And the look he could see, feel, on Fatima's face as she watched him eat and make conversation: Why am *I* not born to such elegant parents. And he himself, later, telling himself over and over, and to Zera: "Why step foot into a world in which we don't belong?"

A world in which he didn't belong? Wasn't she the daughter of his own brother, Akber, who had been caned twenty-five times by their father for serenading a Hindu cobbler's daughter.

His ruminations, having faltered from anxiety to frustration, found relief finally in a happy recollection, and he broke into a wry smile. It had happened one day at work and had been truly uncanny. A thunderbolt from the past.

12

He had been having lunch. The cafeteria at the Ontario Addiction Centre, not very big, at some seventy by thirty feet, is pleasant with many windows and plants and divides roughly at lunchtime into smokers' and nonsmokers' sections. In one the doctors and most of the administrative staff sit, and in the other, the rest.

Nurdin saw an Indian woman in a green sari, middle-aged, of medium height, slim though generously hipped. She walked past him with her tray and he stared. Romesh, sitting with him, also stared. You didn't see many Indians here, and when you saw one, a middle-aged woman, you naturally felt curious and empathized. He stared long, he couldn't help it. There were strong lines on her face and her hair was greying. She sat alone at a table by the windows and after her meal smoked one cigarette. She looked vaguely familiar, he thought he had seen her somewhere, perhaps at an Indian grocery store on Gerrard Street.

It turned out that she was a patient. And every day at lunchtime he looked at her.

"You fancy her?" Romesh asked one day.

"I tell you I've seen her somewhere. What's she in for?"

"Smoking. Looks like one of her allowed daily smokes she's enjoying there," Romesh said. "I hear she's leaving today." Nurdin continued to look at the woman.

"You better find out quick if you want to know who she is," Romesh added.

And Nurdin did. Because, after smoking her cigarette and crushing the stub, she turned sideways on her chair, lifted the hem of her sari ever so slightly to look at a shoe.

And he knew. She was the cobbler's daughter, Sushila, for whom his brother Akber had been whipped senseless! Who had played with him because he was much younger, by five years, who had in fact even come to their house when Akber had gone. He was positive, elated at having made the discovery. Quickly, before she got up, he walked to her table. And stood there.

"How are you, Nurdin Bhai," she said.

"You know – you recognized. . . . " He sat down.

"You know, Nurdin Bhai, you stared so hard at me all these days, it would have been a wonder if I hadn't noticed. You look the same." She smiled.

"Much older."

"Of course, aren't we all."

She was a widow, with a daughter at university, and she lived a short distance away, above a store in Kensington Market. They exchanged pleasantries mostly, that day, exclaiming several times at the wonder of meeting again in such a fashion after such a long time.

"Come home," she said finally, "even by losing your way sometime." She used an old turn of phrase.

"We will, we will. And you come, too, with your daughter."

All afternoon he was excited by the discovery, he couldn't contain himself. He even told Romesh the story about her father Narandas who procrastinated over his customers' shoes until they threatened to go elsewhere – a story which had fallen flat once with the manager of Eatons' shoe department – and Romesh chuckled. "You had those kinds too, eh? So did we!"

Then he went home, saying nothing about his great discovery.

One afternoon, about a week later, Sushila returned to the centre to pick up something, and met Nurdin and Romesh. Actually she had come looking for them. Or Nurdin. She gave him her address – wrote it down for him – and invited them both to tea the following day. "It won't take long. I'll have it ready, just eat and leave. That's the best I can do in honour of our meeting here. You found me out!"

As arranged, at five the next day Nurdin and Romesh stepped out from work and set off for Kensington Market. They walked fast, conspiratorially, as they might have as young boys on a secret mission, to an unpicked mango tree for instance. The apartment, as she had said, was above one of the fruit-and-vegetable stores. Mangoes were few and expensive here, so they settled for oranges instead to take upstairs.

The room they entered was unpretentious, unambitious. No wall-to-wall carpeting, TV console, glass-topped tables. The sofa was a creaky-springed chesterfield, on which they sat a little uncomfortably at first. There were two hard-backed chairs, a table in a corner on which were some books. The first instinct of the two men was pity for the poor creature who had still a long way to go, who didn't as yet know how to live comfortably in Canada. But their hostess was cheerful and gracious. She wore a sari as before. As she had promised, the tea was waiting, and she had managed to obtain a variety of snacks. This first time the talk was small and hurried, a little guarded, a little awkward. This experience, two men visiting a woman alone in her home, was a novel one, for each of them. They talked of rents and prices. Romesh offered financial advice on savings.

Nurdin told his cobbler joke once more and that eased the atmosphere somewhat. Sushila had had better luck than Nurdin at the shoe stores. She was finishing her high school diploma, she said, at which the two men threw a glance at the books on the table in the corner.

"Come again," she said as the men stood up to leave.

"We will, we will," they both said.

"Nurdin Bhai, I hope to see you again," she said at the door, with a smile.

"You come home too," he said, returning her look and feeling very shy at the special attention.

Nurdin and Romesh walked towards the bus stop, subdued and introspective. Nurdin still couldn't get over the coincidence of meeting her. After so long, and in just this little corner of the world! Old memories of the shop on Market Street and the two flats above it, flashed into his mind. He turned towards Romesh to tell him something, at which point Romesh suddenly broke the silence.

"Nur, man, I hope you know. The girl likes you!"

"She'd better. We played together, you know – "

"And you can do the same now. . . . "

"That's unfair, Rom! That's unfair! She's a respectable woman – like a sister."

"Sorry, Nur," said Romesh, taken aback.

After that day, Nurdin would occasionally make a detour to Kensington Market on his way home to buy something or the other, and he would add a little extra detour to go and see Sushila. A short visit for a cup of tea, a little chat. He found he could talk to her, felt the need to go and do just that, even for a few minutes – such a luxury it was, for so long he had had no one to simply sit down and chat with.

They talked about the past, her life, her daughter. An overall impression gradually formed of her, getting more detailed every time he saw her.

She had married quite early, when she was seventeen, to the son of another Dar cobbler. But her husband did not join the family calling and ran a tailoring shop instead. They had a daughter and no other children. No boys. After the country's independence, like others, they had to choose whether to keep their British status or to renounce it. To escape his family's taunts, they chose the former, they went to England. A corner store in London. Meanwhile, several miscarriages. An unhappy, unfulfilled husband who refused to adjust to London. They had never worked so hard before, known so much misery, felt so lost. After her husband died, Sushila refused to go back to Dar or to India, both for her own sake and her daughter's.

"I was not going to slave for my fat mother-in-law and the fat aunts and grandmother. And I would not choose that life for my daughter either. So by and by we heard about Toronto."

And the difference between London and Toronto?

She smiled. "One day I'll tell you."

Her parents were both alive and in India, having saved enough to retire. The little girl, her sister with whom he used to play, was also in India. Her brother was in Dar.

He told her about his family's Montreal trip, about Akber's daughter, the diamond business in Europe. She was highly amused.

"Don't I bring good luck now! Diamonds! If not for me, where would he be now? A bus driver?"

"You know, we are called chammars, low caste, because we handle leather," she told him on one occasion.

He recalled her father, old Narandas, sitting on the floor of his wide-open shop, absorbed, stretching a piece of leather around a dummy foot gripped between the soles of his feet, hammering in the tacks with the little hammer. A short thin man with a scraggly beard, working hard morning to night. Boys would sometimes tease the cobbler, setting firecrackers outside their store.

"To us, all Hindus were the same," Nurdin said. "We called them Banyas – not to my father, of course. He came from the old country, he could tell between the different castes and whatever."

"Now if I had been a Patel or a Shah, a lawyer's or a doctor's daughter, or one of the downtown wholesalers', I might have been acceptable then. He wouldn't have been so harsh on your brother. . . . "

"No, you're wrong there," he said definitely.

"No?"

"No. It would have made no difference. Religion – *din* – came first with him, not status. Even Nehru's Indira would have made no difference to him."

She laughed heartily. "You know, Nurdin Bhai, you have such a sense of humour. You should let it out and laugh."

"Don't I laugh?"

"Yes, but not enough."

She was so charming, he thought, and even at this age so attractive. Was it any wonder Akber had recited ghazals for her and sent a love letter, the first one already with a proposal of marriage? What would he himself have done? He remembered he had also liked her, as a child. *Sushila, Sushila, come play with us.*

"What are you thinking about, Nurdin Bhai?"

He grinned sheepishly. " 'Sushila, Sushila, come play with us.' "

"You remember a lot, Nurdin Bhai."

"Don't call me 'Bhai.' Please."

"Mr. Lalani, then?" She smiled mischievously, expectantly, at him, with a tilt of her head.

"Nurdin."

"Nurdin."

Didn't he laugh enough? Her remark to that effect concerned him for some days. What did she mean? Did he look sad? He always thought of himself as a jolly fellow, though not a loud person.

The fact that she was studying for a high school diploma was also of concern to him. He had never thought, even once, of doing the same. He'd just never thought of it. And here she was – a woman – a humble cobbler's daughter – on her way to getting one. "Why?" he had once asked her.

"I don't know. . . . I always wanted to finish school, but I was not allowed to. Now I will."

"And after that, you'll go to university?" He attempted to sound facetious.

"Maybe. Why not? Let's see. I always dreamed of becoming a lawyer and fighting cases."

With her, he found he could talk. He told her many things: about his kids, his wife, his escapades with Romesh, stopping short of the visit to the peep show – but even that, or something like that, she guessed. She seemed to understand him completely, and her responses were in a language, an idiom, a tone of voice that to him were so perfectly empathetic.

13

It was Saturday night. A sleek white Mercedes was parked right in the driveway of Sixty-nine Rosecliffe Park, close to a lamp and already stuck with a violation ticket. What's a mere fine to a Mercedes owner? And what is a Mercedes for if not to flaunt, under a light here in the front driveway, instead of back in the visitors' area in the company of rusted junks raised up on stones. The prominent licence plate, at the back: JAMAL.

The driveway looked rather mysterious and exotic in the night, its relief of trees, shrubs, and hedges, and the lamps, glowing spheres suspended on relatively short poles, forming areas of alternate darkness and soft light.

As the Lalanis were not in yet, the only place Jamal could be was at the open house on the eighteenth floor. There Nanji found him, patiently but loudly explaining a fine point of the Canadian immigration laws.

The residents of Sixty-nine – those who had been invited – had never forgiven Jamal his wedding reception, where they had been thrown together with people they could not relate to, all the accommodation – including the speech and jokes – being made for those others (the "Canadians") and not for them. They had been made to feel inferior. A new Jamal was expected and had duly come back. No more did he tolerate the old familiarity, the tea-shop mode of greeting: Eh, Jamal, what do you say, wife-kids, urine-water, everything okay, isn't it? What should I do about such and such? To which Jamal, always intimidatingly well dressed, would yield the coolest response. Hi there, Abdul. Meet my spouse. Why don't you come to our office? We'll have a chat and discuss your problem. And the petitioner – with the first available excuse (Oh, there's my wife, nice seeing you) – would escape.

Jamal disliked being treated as one of them, to be identified with the ragamuffin he'd been as a boy, "The Persian" with whom they had played marbles on the sidewalks and cricket in the backyards. For a brief period he had acquired status, in Dar, then he'd lost it. Now, again, after hard work he had status, and they'd better recognize it, these Shamsis from Dar. There was a proper distance between a lawyer and a client. Professional conduct demanded it. He maintained this distance by putting between himself and them a secretary, a saucy "Canadian," who recognized no relationship bar that of lawyer and client. And if they did manage to get past her, they would be confronted with the primly perfect English accent of Jamal's wife Nancy, calling herself Nasim. They knew as well, these Abduls, that if they came to his office, he would charge them by the hour.

"Ah, Nanji – just the person. We were driving by and thought we'd look you up."

Before they could get up, Nanji quickly ordered tea and samosas, which came almost instantly. He consumed them sitting on the floor next to a group playing cards.

The Jamals, on the couch, had resisted so far, though the smells must have tantalized. Now they joined in. "Eh, chacha, what about me?" said Jamal.

"But we thought," began the chacha, throwing a quick glance at Nancy-Nasim – "Oh, sorry, then – "

"Since when have I stopped eating samosas?"

Later the three of them walked out, towards the elevator.

"Nanji, you should have come to our Canada Day party. We missed you."

"The Lalanis – "

"Ah, the Lalanis."

"Well, the kids, then. They asked me to go with them."

"Later I'll tell you about our friend, Nurdin. I say, why don't you come back with us now, you could spend the night."

"Yes, do," said Nasim.

He had already stayed overnight at their fashionable apartment downtown. But Nanji decided, never again. He would not be adopted, nor give them the opportunity to indulge in pitying him, when it was they who needed him, probably had nothing to do tonight, had missed out on some invitation or another.

"No, thanks," Nanji said. Then, "Why don't you come sit at my place, you've not seen it for a while."

"From what I have heard . . . " said Nasim Jamal playfully.

"It's different now."

When they walked in to Nanji's apartment, they were impressed. Jamal gave his characteristic whoop. "Wow, man! This is it. Now you are beginning to live. Come out of your shell, Nanji, and you and I will hit this town hard – "

"All this in honour of the girls! Nanji, you've surpassed yourself," said Nasim.

Nanji was never sure how to respond to her. He would have to get used to her. He wondered how much she simply tolerated him for her husband's sake. Jamal had chosen wisely, having taken good measure of his weaknesses. She was the counterweight, the anchor to his wild fancies. And probably the reason why he would succeed. But in what?

"Nanji, you should have brought them *home*."

"Well, you know how these girls are. Hardly time to pause."

"So, you had a good time." Jamal grinned at him enviously. He grinned back.

"And at what stage have you reached in your long – I should say your epic – romance?" Jamal went on.

He could never resist a little jibe, to stay on top, even though he didn't expect this answer.

"Finished."

"Finished?"

"Dead."

Nanji composed himself, bringing out a bottle of wine and glasses.

"But you look good – doesn't he, dear?"

"I should say so."

Jamal briefly held his glance, looking for signs of any damage he might have done.

You had to admit, Nanji thought, he was not without compassion. Why do I like him so, this crude, insolent guy, presumptuous . . . even at his most polished you cannot but see the jagged roughness. If there is anyone worth watching, any life worth following, it's surely his. Even in his conformity, his assumed respectability, he is taking a risk, walking the dangerous path – and he knows it! He knows the risk.

"You look good, Nanji."

"It had to end. It just wasn't right – like taking the wrong road and afraid to get off."

"Now you're off. I'm glad. We have things to do together."

Jamal sipped his wine, sat back, and took out a cigarette, saying "May I?" to his wife, who nodded indulgently. "You're something, Nanji - keeping wine in this building where God lurks in every corridor. And they know it, these friends of yours. If it were me" - he sipped - "I would be condemned by the Grand Sheriff of Mecca."

They grinned at each other.

"I've been to Dar - personal," Jamal said quietly.

"You've been to Dar! You were not afraid?"

"Shitless, at first. But I had to go one more time."

"So how is your father?"

"Mellow - but will not come to Canada. Sister's married, has a shop. So much for my family."

"And how was *Dar*?"

"Finished. But let me tell you who I saw. In Dar I saw" - he took a deep puff of his cigarette and tapped the ashes into an ashtray with flourish while Nanji reminded himself of his friend's dramatic career - "none other than our former resident - "

"Esmail."

"Esmail. And guess what he's doing?"

"Painting."

"He is in an artists' colony just outside Dar, one of its main attractions."

"Wow. So he found a place for himself."

"And how. Students - American students, nice pretty girls - go and study this art. They write about it. Next month representatives of the colony are going to an exhibition and conference in New York – East African retrospective or something. And Esmail will be there. He is painting nothing but masks now. He showed me."

"So how can Dar be finished when it can do that?"

"Dar didn't do it – Canada did."

"By breaking his legs, you mean."

"I didn't quite mean that, but there's that too."

"I was there."

Esmail the baker, kneeling on the tracks, crying hoarsely, Save me! Save me! his meat pies strewn over the platform. Perhaps *he* will be the great success. We'll buy UNESCO cards with his paintings on them. While those immigrant Toronto poets and artists having periodic jubilees in the streets rot, out of context, their roots out in the cold – irrelevant to the world, any world, marginal. . . .

"And listen," Jamal was saying, "I've brought the most exquisite zebra skin with me – not easy, you know, there are new laws. You must come and see. . . . "

Jamal was quickly becoming a big success as a lawyer. His cases were getting to be known. And there were hordes of people seeking immigration advice, people trying to bring families into Canada. Many of his clients were businessmen who could afford to pay thousands of dollars. People who were not his type, he reminded Nanji. "Wait," he said to his friend, reiterating an old promise, "wait until

I've made my millions. Then I'll do something great." But then it could be too late, thought Nanji to himself, and immediately censured himself for becoming a grapeless fox.

Nasim-Nancy was getting restless. In her home, she would simply have fallen asleep on the rug.

"We should come more often now," she began, with a look at her husband.

He took the cue, they stood up to leave.

"You were going to tell me about Nurdin," said Nanji, standing up.

"Ah, yes. Listen to this. Our friend was seen at a peep show."

"You must be kidding. Are you sure? Where?"

"Yonge Street, where else? My client works there – and knows him."

"Nice clients you have."

"At least they work. Well, what do you have to say to that?"

"I don't know. Once he asked me if eating pork could change one's character."

"So our Mr. Lalani is being tempted by this devil of a world. You think we should warn him and save his soul?"

They were at the door. There was that look in Jamal's eyes, sizing you up, and a shadow of a smile on his wide mouth.

"N-no. He's his own man."

His own man. And the kids and Zera? But Nurdin deserved a chance to find his own way, Nanji figured. Even if he risked hurting himself.

14

Nurdin Lalani had once been enthusiastic about his new home – the setting up, the new possibilities, the children's future. Even the hardships gave a romantic aspect to the whole endeavour. But no more, he thought. He found it difficult to set his heart on his home. It seemed drawn out *there* – out the balcony, across the valley, and towards the city. . . .

Gone were the days of fullness of heart, the sense of wholeness at having children. Time was when it was children that brought a man rushing home. From work. From travels. But this country had taken his children away, and he felt distanced, rejected by them. Especially the girl.

There were times when, he was sure, she despised him. For what he was, unsophisticated, uneducated, a peon. For the crime of being her father when he wasn't anything like what she had in mind. She was ashamed of this little Paki-shitty-stan of Don Mills, as she called it. She didn't belong here, she would pull herself out of this condition: everything about her attitude suggested that. She would rise to where they had neither the courage nor the ability to reach. Where had she picked up this abrasiveness, this shrillness, this hatred of her origins? "I will be president of IBM," she would announce, more to taunt, he believed, than anything else. "But you want to do pharmacy," he once ventured. "Okay, president of Dupont Chemicals," she retorted. "The president of Dupont is probably someone already called Dupont," said Nanji, who was at the table.

One day, when she was younger, Nurdin had gone to her school to pick up her grades. A single B had bothered him, though he could have lived with it. But she would have sulked all day, so he went to talk to her teacher. "It's all right," she said. "It's a course that doesn't matter." "Even then," he said. She changed it. Then, as he was leaving, she called, "Bye, doctor." There was no one else there, he stopped in his tracks and turned around. She saw the look on his face and said, "What's the matter, aren't you a doctor?" "No," he replied. "Well, Fatima always talks about her doctor father." That was one of the few wringers their little Fatima had put them through.

He was grateful to Nanji for having made that remark, defusing the situation. She was in awe of

Nanji. How much so, Nanji himself wasn't aware of, being under the impression that her wearing dresses now and more fashionable clothes meant she no longer thought much of him. But that remark of his had cut her to the quick.

Always in a hurry, she had skipped a year in high school and had applied to several universities. Soon she would be off, and glad to be away. She would never miss her father. She would mellow surely, but not before she had gone through a few more years of life . . . quite a few more. Nurdin always found it unfair that although she would laugh at her mother, she still liked her. Because her mother had been a student and a teacher. That was one more thing against him, he had brought her mother to *this*.

Then there was Hanif, a little monkey until recently, who had caused no end of embarrassments. His voice had started to change, and he had shot up as tall as his sister and was still growing. She would need him. He was the stronger of the two and not only physically. Hanif was a good boy. He had respect and he was quietly spoken. But he didn't really need anybody. He liked to talk to Nanji, though, whom he called Eeyore. He would seek out Nanji and get him talking. And then afterwards, feeling his sister's envy, he would talk about what Eeyore had said.

They were waiting for the Master, Missionary, whose departure from Dar was imminent. He was waiting for tickets and passports and foreign exchange, all to be acquired illegally for him by Nurdin's own younger brother, Shamshu. One brother making millions in the diamond business, the other making his – so Nurdin had heard – in the black market. Always he, Nurdin, the middle one, neither here nor there.

He was sitting in his armchair, looking out; Zera was on the phone making one of numerous arrangements for Missionary; in the distance, in front of him, the CN Tower blinked constantly in the darkness. At times like these, all to himself, he would on occasion think of the old days . . . of his stern old father who had terrified him so much . . . of his brothers and sisters and the family . . . of his schooldays . . . of his buddy, Charles, and the days and nights they spent in the forest together on their way to sell Bata shoes. Charles was the only person he'd come really close to, in his life there, to whom he opened his heart. And he a black man. Those times in the forest, on the road, were what he treasured most out of his memories. They were moments he could truly call all his own.

There was one scene that came vividly to his mind, often, when he sat in his armchair, watched the CN Tower, and let his mind wander. It took place one midafternoon. He and Charles had cooked some maizemeal and beans under an ancient tree, and, while eating, quiet and absorbed, something had made them both look up. They saw an eerie sight that shattered their peace, that sent a shiver up Nurdin's spine. They were being watched. Some fifty yards away stood a group of people, black people in rags, in loose formation. Looking strange in the distance, waiting and watching, silent and intimidating . . . until suddenly the details of the men, women, and children registered horribly, in Nurdin's mind. Thin, emaciated, the women with sagging breasts and exhausted looks; the children with flies buzzing around their noses, eyelids, and sores; old, pathetic grey-haired men shorn of all dignity – all patiently waiting. From time to time someone would go to take a drink from a muddy puddle. The area was suffering a drought, he recalled. Nauseated, feeling the hungry eyes on every morsel of food he tried to raise to his mouth or swallow, he could not finish the meal. And finally, when he and Charles walked up to the dump to throw the leftovers, they were surrounded by a swarm of children begging for the remains. To this day he could not recall what he had done. Perhaps he'd let his plate be snatched away by the nearest and fastest pair of hands. It was a memory that tugged at his heart.

In Toronto's Dar immigrant gatherings it was considered positively uncouth to recall with any seriousness that previous life. Not quite realizing this, he had on one or two occasions attempted to point out a minute detail, something precious that brought out the nuance of a life once lived, only to be scorned by the grinning mouth of his sister-in-law, This-Is-Canada Roshan. Of course, the Shamsis of Dar had recreated their community life in Toronto: the mosques, the neighbourhoods, the clubs, and the associations. They even had the Girl Guides, with the same troop leaders as in Dar. But no Boy Scouts: some things were different. That was the whole crux of the matter now. Their Dar, however close they tried to make it to the original, was not quite the same. Rushing to mosque after work in your Chevy, through ice and slush, for a ceremony organized in a school gym, dumping your coats on a four-foot mound of other coats and throwing your shoes and boots among the several hundred other pairs – and then afterwards scrambling to retrieve them – was not the same as strolling to your own domed, clock-towered mosque fresh after a bath.

More than this – more than appearances – the sparkle was missing. That intangible that lights up the atmosphere – the spirit, perhaps – was missing, as everyone, even Roshan This-Is-Canada acknowledged. All this said was that they, themselves, waiting for their master, Missionary, to come and reinforce their faiths, were also not quite the same.

And he, how much had he changed? Had he changed enough . . . and for what purpose? Out the balcony and across the valley his thoughts flew, to her.

He had gone early this time to Sushila so he could be there a little longer. As he turned onto her street and approached the market, he saw her take a momentary glance down from the first-floor window and then withdraw. He walked up the ancient wooden stairs at the side of the two-storey building. They made an incredible racket. The door upstairs was unlatched, as he expected, and he walked in. She had gone back into the bedroom and he sat down in the living room to wait. Moments later she appeared at the doorway between the two rooms, in the midst of draping a sari around her. There was a safety pin between her lips. The sari was green and white, the blouse a dark green, opaque. Holding the folds in place at her waist with one hand, she raised the other to take the pin. Already, a little wet patch in the armpit. From this sideways pose she looked angular, the neck taut, the bun of hair small and hard at the back. Strands of white above the ear. Not a word yet exchanged between them. He had helped himself to the tea from the waiting pot.

An exclamation, *tch*, then the folds loosened, the pin went back between the lips, the freed hand arrived too late to prevent the sari from unwinding by the loose end. The slip, opaque, of the same material as the blouse.

The sari enhances the hips, really gives shape to a woman, he thought, watching her closely.

The process was repeated, and when she had wound the sari round the waist and hips, she said, "Nurdin, I think you'll have to come and help me with this pin."

His teacup did a nervous tattoo on the saucer and he firmly pressed them together.

"It's okay. I got it." She looked up brightly, coming into the living room finally, walking gracefully, the sari in place. "It's not easy to put on, you know. You men have it easy."

"But it's worth the trouble. It looks good."

There was a freedom in her, a wholeness, a self-sufficiency. Drudgery had not destroyed her charm, and here she was, almost intact. From such a woman you can learn much. With someone like her you could do anything, not be afraid to go anywhere. He realized the illegitimacy of the thought, the hidden desire it contained.

"What are you thinking?"

"I am thinking how different you are from other women."

"When you're a widow you learn to cope."

"Don't you get lonely . . . when your daughter is away?"

"Yes. I tried to gas myself once . . . with my daughter. In London."

"What happened then?"

"I woke up. Found her looking out of the window at the snow falling. Christmas Eve. For some, God comes down on that night bearing gifts. For others, there's nothing in the world. I've learned to live with myself, but I enjoy company, as you can see."

He was silent. It was as if he had taken a deep dive underwater and come up a little dazed. He wondered how much more there was to her.

"You asked the wrong question," she said, at length. "Tell you what. Let's go downstairs. I want to do some shopping. I've invited some people for dinner."

She seemed to know all the shopkeepers downstairs, for some of them she had worked before. There were similarities in what they would buy, of course, but now and then, with a knowing smile she would pick up something that was a total surprise – and a source of delight – for him, like a vegetable he didn't know the name of. This pointed to her different upbringing, of course. To be a Hindu you have to know your vegetables. He found on the other hand that she did not like to spend time buying meat, and he had to help her.

Mission accomplished, they sat down at the bakery. It was running late for Nurdin, but today he could make an exception.

She was looking earnestly at him. "Nurdin, I would like to tell you something."

"Shoot," he said, using an expression he had learned from Romesh and feeling rather good.

"You know, Nurdin – forgive me – but the time at which you come . . . it's a little awkward."

"I'm sorry if I've disturbed you."

His heart sank. Just when his life had received a spark, just when he was feeling the best he had felt in a long, long time.

"Oh, no. Please don't misunderstand me. I do like you to come. But, you know, I never know *when* you're coming."

"I figured if you were not in, I would go away."

"That wastes your time, doesn't it? Makes you late at home for no reason. Why don't you call before, and come for a longer time. This way I feel like I'm running a tea shop."

They both laughed.

"Listen. Why don't you take the afternoon off, Monday week. It'll be fun. Hunh?"

He had not made the proposition, she had. By it, his thirty-minute stolen visits had been shorn of all innocence, the pretence of teatime chitchat. He could go forward or step back, there was no neutral ground, had never been one. What to do? Let his life slip by, this golden opportunity escape – for what? He was a mere servant, slaving away for his children, whose lives now all lay before them, full of possibilities – did they really need him any more? And Zera was wedded to God, it seemed. If he procrastinated, he would never do it, never break these chains which bound him to a term of work and service to which no end was in sight. Sushila promised release. She was waiting for him, he only had to give the word . . . simpler, only had to take the Monday afternoon off and go to her. She needed him, sure. But she was not a whore. A little free, perhaps. But wasn't it this freedom that was so attractive, that made possible a new world – his own freedom?

He had begun looking more at himself, become aware of his looks, took greater care with them. He used a simple ruse at home to carry this through: "Eti, Zera, do you think I look scruffy? The director of the centre wants me to dress up. . . . " So easily it came, this deception. He explained it to himself by saying that he hated explanations. A simple friend, yet talking about her would raise all kinds of complications. A simple friend? Now the time had come to choose. The simple phase of his friendship had ended.

Lately he was avoiding Zera's eyes, although he was certain she could never fathom what lay behind his. With the kids it was different: they were always in a hurry, had no time for anyone but themselves. There was that photo on the wall, those eyes that bore into the sides of his head, digging up guilty secrets. And that constant abstract signal in the distance, from the concrete god who didn't care.

The local chapter of Missionary's followers, a group of women, had started regular evening meetings at the Lalanis'. They discussed and meditated, but mostly they liked to discuss. Sometimes they sang late into the night, so that he would wake up to humming sounds he wasn't sure were in his head or outside – until he turned to check if Zera was beside him. And now there were three boys, whom Zera had found. One had volunteered to be the Master's chauffeur for as long as he was needed. The second one collected and classified all the tapes of the Master's talks. Nurdin hadn't figured out the third one yet.

15

The rubber-tiled floors of the Ontario Addiction Centre are spotless and the walls are plain white, as would suit the look of a medical institution. But the corridors in this square building on the main floor face an open courtyard with windows all along their sides; this, with an abundance of well-situated greenery on both sides of the windows, and the loud, cheerful voices, particularly those of the doctors, make it generally a bright and pleasant place.

The basement level, quiet and windowless, is bright and gleaming in artificial light. It houses the supply rooms. From one of them Nurdin Lalani emerged at eleven o'clock one morning, a few days after his last visit to Sushila. He was pushing a squeaking trolley heaped with bed linen. The door clicked shut behind him, and he turned a corner and pushed towards the elevators. As he approached the small lobby facing the two elevators, he saw in front of him a girl in blue jeans sitting on the floor, leaning against the side wall. Her legs were drawn up in front of her, her hands hung limp on the raised knees, and her head was lowered. Obviously she had been crying, the blonde hair was dishevelled, the face – what he could see of it – was puffy and red.

Instinctively he hurried towards her, parking the trolley on the way. "Madam – Miss – is anything wrong? Can I be of any help?"

There was no response. He looked up again, turned around, there was no one coming. He tried again. "Miss, shall I call a doctor?"

He was almost squatting beside her now, his hand was on her shoulder. He realized he had never been so close to a white woman before. And he realized he had become aware of her femaleness. He caught, quite strongly, the whiff of creamy makeup. Her blouse was white, embroidered at the neck. A button was open and he could see the curve of a breast. The skin there was pale, almost white, and dull. He was waiting for her to respond to his offer of help.

The response, when it came, was not quite what he expected. His hand was still on her shoulder when suddenly she gave the alarm.

"RAPE!" she cried. "He's trying to rape me!"

Nurdin got up. "Heh-heh-heh," he laughed. "You had me fooled." For the first time their eyes met. Hers flashed with anger. He felt nervous as he backed away, the situation looked threatening. He pressed the elevator button and got in, without the trolley, as she was still yelling "RAPE! Help, someone!" There was an oppressive empty feeling in the pit of his stomach which was to stay with him for a long time to come.

He went to find Romesh and told him all about it. They concluded that the matter couldn't be serious, the girl was probably an outpatient drug addict who would calm down.

They always took their lunch late, after one o'clock. In the cafeteria that day, pushing his tray along the counter behind Romesh, he came face to face with the server, short Mrs. Broadbent, hair inside a net, fiery eyes glaring at him behind glasses with open hostility, hands at her waist.

"There he is – you shameless man!"

His heart sank and he became truly fearful.

She had liked him at first, calling him "dear," until once he had asked – half in jest – for a larger piece of choice meat obviously reserved for a "boss," one of the male doctors or administrators. From then on, a glaring eye was his lot, his piece flopped on the plate. This had been a source of great amusement to him and Romesh. Now she had her revenge.

"I'm not going to serve this rapist!" she said, turning away.

"I thought in this country a man was innocent until proved guilty," said Romesh, to no one in particular.

"Where he comes from, both his hands would be chopped off," announced Mrs. Broadbent. "Yes, and – "

"And his marbles too," added Romesh.

The West Indian cook served Nurdin.

As they went to sit down, everyone present, it seemed, turned to look at him. He tried to eat, wondering what would happen next.

"I think I'll go and explain to the director," he told Romesh desperately. The incident loomed larger than he had thought was possible. How could a girl make an accusation and have everyone believe her. He should not have walked away. He should have stayed and defended himself, there and then.

They were still drinking their coffee, slowly, there were a few people around. It was not yet two o'clock when two policemen showed their faces at the door, short Mrs. Broadbent dead centre between them.

He was asked to accompany the policemen.

"If I'm not back by five, call my wife," he said to Romesh.

He had touched her, and he had an indecent thought about her – was that enough to qualify as rape? There was that guilty thought and perhaps . . . perhaps during that instant of which he could recall nothing, perhaps then he did do something. But no. If he had touched her breast, he would know, he would feel it on his hand, the place where it had touched her. His hands felt pure, only his mind had deviated. He should not have walked away.

And besides, he had approached her with the purest of intentions, had shown concern. He had heard long ago that in America you did not touch a person even if they were dying and needed help. Why should Canada be different. He should have known better.

In the police car he was vaguely conscious of passing shop signs. When it slowed or stopped at intersections, he would sit well back, hunched, to avoid curious eyes.

He could be dreaming. His mind, outside this one event, felt numb. Nothing from that other world could be remotely connected to his present condition, which should be able to resolve itself, disappear, like a dream when one wakes up.

At the station he protested his innocence. "I only tried to help her." "I have a daughter her age, would I do such a thing?" He sobbed. He had to wait a long time after the initial questioning. Some people were brought in to look at him, and he realized he had become a suspect for other crimes as well. His face was compared to some drawings that two policemen brought and studied but kept away from him. A plainclothesman watched a videotape and studied him closely at the same time. He was asked to speak into a telephone, and knew that even his voice was under scrutiny. Finally he was booked for indecent assault on one Maria Viviana Baptista of Kensington Avenue and given a date on which to appear in court.

16

He had felt crushed when he came home from the police station. To face your wife and have to tell her: "They say I attacked a girl." Not meet her eyes because there was that other guilt, the guilt of all his little misdemeanours, and the guilt of visiting another woman, planning a tryst. . . .

Then Hanif had asked, "Did you?" And Zera had asked, "Did you?"

Did they have such little faith in him – did they believe him capable of anything – and could he really blame them now? In bed she once half turned towards him to ask: "You didn't actually do it, did you?" He remained silent, looking up at the ceiling.

The sound of the television was faintly audible: the kids unable to sleep. . . . Fatima all charged up thinking of her father's folly and how it would affect her future. He had by now learned of her own little disaster – Arts and Science instead of Pharmacy. "Weren't you tempted?" Zera asked.

"I was tempted. . . . I wasn't tempted. . . . I didn't do it."

The following days he wasn't himself, wasn't there, at all. It was, every time he became conscious of his situation, as if he had taken a tremendous fall, then getting up, not knowing how much of him was still there intact. Most of the time there was this heaviness in the heart, pulling him inside, into himself, making him inattentive, vague, numb, as if what he suffered from was something terribly physical, the aftermath of a deafening explosion, whose echoes drove everything else from his mind, made discussion meaningless. Only his lawyer Jamal could extract some response from him.

Missionary's arrival, a week after the incident, turned out to be a blessing, although Nurdin had not really looked forward to it. Amidst the comings and goings, the telephone ringing, and a multitude of problems, petitions and requests submitted daily, his own problem receded into the background for him to agonize over in his private moments, to emerge only now and then when attention was drawn to him. And the Master had such a sense of humour, to which Nurdin could readily respond. He found himself very much at ease with the Master. Zera, in a weepy moment stolen from the hustle and bustle, had indicated to him that her heart was heavy, there was a problem in the family: "No, not the children – Nurdin." He called Nurdin over, asked him the facts, and then said, "It will be all right," which pronouncement relieved Zera considerably. In fact, for her, the problem was solved that instant.

Nanji was present when Missionary made his first visit to the Lalanis', accompanied by the newly acquired retinue of young men, in front, behind, and beside, and awaited by his congregation sitting on the floor in the living room. His wife and daughter made up the tail end of the procession. The sofa against the wall was the seat of honour, in front of which all sat waiting. As he entered the room the females of the congregation, dressed in white, attempted an elaborate welcoming ceremony, with touching of feet and cracking of knuckles and garlanding, but in his summary fashion the Master told them to be seated. Not that they minded. Any word from him to them was gold.

It was remarkable, Nanji thought, how much he seemed to have shrunk in physique. The same smile, the oval bald head, the portliness, and the famous light blue suit. But somehow, it was as if the bones had settled into a more compact form. Or was it that the old world now looked small and fragile?

As he sat down on the sofa he called out play-fully, "Eh, Nurdin. I see you've installed a goddess in your building, downstairs. Where is the god?"

Nurdin, standing near the window, played along, gesturing at the Master in mock seriousness. "Come, Missionary, I will show you."

The Master, with a smile and a twinkle in his eye, got up and walked through the congregation and stood beside Nurdin. "There," said Nurdin, pointing out the window into the distance. "There is our god. But he is a deep one. Mysterious."

The Master chuckled. "Ah, the CN Tower. I have been to the top of it, many years ago. Excellent restaurant."

Sitting down again he called his wife beside him. His daughter was also pushed forward by the crowd. She was tall and fair and her hair was cut short. She wore a loose shirt over her brown cordu-roy jeans. Her name was Khadija – not one of those fancy Persian flower-names so much in vogue but a respectable traditional one. Unfortunately this was also the name much favoured by the older genera-tion, the grandmothers, who shortened it to Khati. So the girl had to make the best not only of the name but also its short form. Having been brought into the limelight now, all she could do was to put on a pleasant little smile and look at her hands. She didn't last long however under the blissful gazes of the women and found a pretext to go and stand outside in the main passageway, from where, when she looked in, she could catch the proceedings. It seemed that she found enough to divert herself there, in the kitchen perhaps, and showed her face only intermittently.

For quite some time they talked in the Lalanis' living room, of food prices and currency values "there," of who was "in" (for black-marketing and passport violations) and who "out." Food prices were rising, there were queues for bread, garbage was not being picked up regularly. It was as if they had to justify living here by proving to themselves how progressively worse it was getting there. Finally someone raised a religious issue. It was the second acolyte.

Nurdin had labelled the three young men: Number One, Number Two, and Number Three. Number One simply gave his services, he was companion and chauffeur and could well have been valet but for the wife. Number Two was archivist and librarian, who fancied himself junior Master. Number Three – no one could quite place him, but sometimes he substituted for Number One. Nice boys all, they gave Missionary hope for the future in Canada.

Number Two had asked a question, having killed the previous topic, and then began answering his own question. To which the Master patiently listened, and then cut in with his own version.

At this point Nanji, who was standing somewhere at the fringe and out of the way, thought it wise to leave. He went through the inner of the two kitchen doorways and emerged at the other end, in the passageway leading out. There, to his dismay, Missionary's daughter, Khati, was standing like a guard.

She quickly moved aside. "Leaving so soon?" she beamed.

"Well. . . . " What excuse to give?

"Have a mind of your own, eh?"

"I prefer to do my own thinking, yes." If that's what she wants to hear. She can report that to her father if she likes.

"There's nothing wrong with that. It's perfectly all right."

The cheek! Now she was patronizing him. "Why, thank you. What about you? You must know it all by heart . . . all this . . . religion."

The smile dimmed. She pouted. "Now you are mocking."

He said nothing.

"All right, go and do your thinking."

"Actually, I am just going to my place to make myself some coffee. Would you like to join me?"

It turned out she was an accountant, but hadn't worked for a year, having spent the time with her parents. She had gone to England after high school, and the accent was there. Obviously a girl no longer in her father's shadow.

"I don't always agree with my father. But he's getting old now. I just go along, for things that really don't matter."

"Like that shirt, for instance?"

"Is it that obvious?" She giggled self-consciously. "He thinks the hips should be covered with a shirt or kurta. I couldn't find anything else."

"But your mother, I thought I saw her in a blouse, tucked in – "

"Well," she said, "I guess he thinks – "

"That" – he caught himself and froze his smile.

"Now don't say what you are thinking!" The giggle again, such a delightful giggle, and he laughed his silent laugh. He would never forget that giggle, he thought.

In the middle of all the excitement in his home, with the Master's comings and goings, Nurdin, suspended from work, was still awaiting his court hearing.

"Do you think he did it?" Nanji had asked Jamal one day.

"For a man who has taken to visiting peep shows, it's not quite unthinkable."

"What will happen?"

"With his record and background – a light reprimand."

"But with a record?"

"With a record. And probably some publicity."

Missionary, who had advice on everything from childrearing to managing a country's economy – in his time he'd been an educated man – had taken to advising Jamal about the case. Jamal simply pocketed the advice and forgot it. Even he couldn't risk offending the old man. The man in his heyday had thrilled thousands, young and old; they had flocked to the mosques to hear him speak. He had been a fiery hot-blooded speaker. "You are all donkeys," he would tell them. But they loved him. "You were low-class Hindu thieves and criminals before you converted," he would yell. They still loved him.

Nanji remembered an instance from his childhood, how one night he had awakened his grandmother after they had both gone to bed, to remind her that Missionary was speaking that night, after months of silence. They got up, dressed, walked the dark streets to go and listen to whatever remained of the sermon. And in school, another time, after having invited Missionary to give his class a talk, Nanji had then gathered enough courage during question period to inquire when an embryo inside a mother acquires a soul. The Master had had an answer for that too. And even to the question whether a dog had a soul. Nanji didn't quite remember what he had said, and he didn't now care.

What was amazing, observing him now after many years, was that the man was so human. He was no ascetic. He liked food, delighted in conveniences and gadgets, and was definitely not one to spurn a car ride in favour of walking out in the cold. His last major battle perhaps had been with his eldest son, chosen to follow in his footsteps, who had however gone against his advice, his command, to let go his American girlfriend and marry someone of the community. This, when hundreds came to seek his advice, whether to marry this girl or that boy, what name to give their child, what to do about this or

that ailment, if the time was ripe for going into business. Even Nurdin and Zera had married upon his
advice. But his own son had turned him down, marrying his American girlfriend. Father and son had
not exchanged a word for some years now. No one,
sitting at the Master's feet, could not have been aware
of his problems. As if to explain their existence, one
day he had given a little "example" to the gathering
before him.

A yogi was practising extreme asceticism in the
forest. He had no possessions, except the knickers
held in place only with a string – Missionary, in his
grave manner, could be rather graphic, and you had
to hide your smile. But, Missionary continued, the
rats in the cave in which the yogi lived would nibble
at the string as he slept. To keep away the rats, the
poor yogi kept a cat. To feed the cat milk, he kept a
cow. And to feed and look after the cow, he had got a
wife. To keep her happy, he had to give her children.

The rapt audience broke into a murmur when
he finished. Acolyte Number One gave a barely audible laugh, and Number Two began comparing this
example with another example. But the Master's
hand was on his wife's back, and he looked around
the room as if he wished he could go somewhere. He
had done this most of his life, keeping such gatherings happy, he couldn't do anything else now. This
is what it would always be. You couldn't help noticing the fondness of the old couple for each other. He
tried to infuse these gatherings with a spirit of infor-
mality, so that the women in white who had started

out by sitting at his feet were now on chairs. At one point Zera and Mrs. Missionary both went to make tea in the kitchen, and Zera came out bringing a cup for him. He responded to this by saying jovially, "I will have tea only from my wife's hands. This cup, you give to Nurdin there." A significant lesson for Zera. She went and sat beside her husband.

At this point Nurdin's problem came to mind, and Missionary entered into a tirade against the morality of Western society, a society whose virtues he had been singing about not long ago. But who said the Master was consistent? He could talk of future generations, and shortly thereafter give you the exact date, forty years and some months from today, when the world would come to an end in an armageddon. It made him human – he had studied a lot from a variety of sources, traditional and modern, so obviously there were loose ends. At one time he was among the few who were educated, he was in step, at least with his world; once he had had contemporaries to discuss and argue with. Now his companions were young people such as Number Two, ranting out of their place, out of their time.

Nanji was getting restless. From a corner Khati saw him squirming, but he expected no sympathy from there. He allowed himself to suffer some more and then made his escape.

If Missionary was human, his daughter was more so. Nanji had already walked to the Rosecliffe Park Mall with her. And together with Fatima and Hanif, he had taken her to the Eaton Centre. He had waited patiently while she went up and down the Marks & Spencer store. He had argued with her and laughed with her . . . let her laugh at him. He liked her. He liked her very much. That conclusion sounded like a death sentence. Just when he had recovered, when he was enjoying himself, yes, in a Buddhistic-existentialist trance (that anecdote about the yogi's knickers was disturbing, though), along had come Life, in the form of this girl. Wasn't Buddha tempted by Mara?

And this girl, a jewel really, she must have someone waiting for her, surely. And there must be countless of her father's rich acquaintances, with doctor-sons who would grab at this combination of East and West, spunk and coyness, given half the chance? Perhaps he needn't worry, she was taken. But those looks and smiles on Zera's face – had he been set up even before Missionary arrived? So what. He dared not contemplate the possibilities. The romantic path is strewn with hazards and heartache, unfulfillable dreams. He wished he *had* been set up.

She was so different from Yasmin: she did not move like a hurricane, yet there was so much of her. You did not have to rush to concerts, parties, plays, recitals, or picnics; you just had to be. She bubbled forth with life, experience, observations, humour. And then, she understood him, his concerns with life, but she was such an antidote to his high-minded seriousness, dissolving it like a potion – some kind of Alka Seltzer, he thought wryly. Can one risk joy in life? Again?

When a woman lets you open your heart to her, well and good, but when she opens her heart to you, beware, for she may turn you into a friend, a *brother*. God, what have I let myself in for this time?

He was getting ready to go to a film. A brisk walk in the clear, moonless night, then a respectably "heavy" film. There would be a discussion at the end, from which he would walk out, again into the cool, starry night, alone with the Universe. At such moments nothing can touch you.

There was a knock and then banging at his door, with accompanying sounds of several pairs of feet and murmurs outside, as if a gang were waiting there to enter. It was Fatima, Hanif – and Khati.

"Hey, looks like you're going to a party," said Hanif, and they all pushed in.

"I'm going to a movie."

"Which movie?"

"Yeah, which one?"

Several names were suggested.

"An Indian film at the Ontario Science Centre. After which there will be a discussion." He sounded sufficiently solemn and nerdy, he thought.

"Can I come," said Khati.

He felt rather irritable. If left alone, he would have survived her. He shooed the other two out and closed the door.

"Look," he said, turning a weary face on her.

"Are you going to beat me?"

"Look – I'm getting tired . . . getting rather fond of you and . . . and I have no time for platonic relationships, fraternity in Islam, and so on." There. He put out his hand for the program she had picked up.

"I'm still coming with you."

"Okay," he said, in a voice intended to carry some threat.

They walked to the elevator in silence. "Tell me about this festival," she said, pointing at the movie program. He muttered something, watching the overhead panel impatiently. He had made up his mind.

They walked outside, to the driveway he liked so much at this time of the night. Her hands were in her jacket pockets, and she was keeping pace with him without attempting to break the silence. Between two shrubs, in a relatively dark spot, he slowed down. Turning a little so he could see, he took her hand and held it inside his. Together, like that, they walked at a brisk pace to go see the movie.

Nurdin realized that by now the knowledge of his accusation was public. From his own home, the discussions with the Master, it must have gone out in waves to the remainder of the community – Don Mills, Willowdale, Scarborough, Mississauga, Bramp-

ton . . . perhaps even Kitchener-Waterloo and soon
Calgary-Vancouver. He wondered if Missionary himself believed him guilty or innocent. Certainly you
could not help feeling that he could see into your
innermost thoughts.

Missionary had brought with him Haji Lalani's
old red fez, the one the old man was wearing when
he died and which had been forgotten in the English
teacher's back seat until Missionary retrieved it. He
pulled quite a surprise on them. Sitting on the sofa
in the Lalanis' apartment Missionary, beaming with
pleasure, told the family to close their eyes, which
they did, wondering if the joke this time would be
funny, because sometimes it wasn't and they had to
humour him. Meanwhile he brought out the fez
from a bag and put it on his own head. "Well, Nurdin," he said, when they opened their eyes, "what
punishment do you deserve?"

Nurdin recoiled, flitting his eyes from his father's hat on the Master's head to his father's picture
on the wall, back and forth, several times. The very
same hat that his father had worn, day in and day
out, before him now, more real than the photograph.
He could touch it and in a sense touch his father,
smell it and catch a whiff of the old man's head, the
hair oil he used. But the Master gave a hearty laugh –
bouncing like a gentle spring with only a quiet
squeak – which brought tears to his eyes.

"Nurdin," he said, wiping his eyes, "does it still
frighten you so?" He removed the hat from his head,
holding it irreverently like the dead object it was, and

he laughed some more and they couldn't help laughing with him. That instant the red fez was exorcized. In one stroke that photograph on the wall had lost all potency, its once accusing eyes were now blank, its expression dumb. Suddenly they were here, in the modern world, laughing at the past.

Jamal had already reassured Nurdin he would not spend the rest of his life in jail, his wife and kids begging in the streets, and so on, as in the Bombay talkies. The most he would get was a reprimand. And a criminal record. "I would stay away from those peep shows, if I were you," he told him.

"But Jamal, I went there once – only once – I swear to you. And I didn't even know what it was – who told you?"

Who else knew? The strange thing was that if they knew about Sushila – the real thing – then they would all believe him, his innocence. Jamal had finally gone away convinced, at least partly, and said he would go and talk to the girl and get her to drop charges.

"Well, Nurdin, by the time this thing blows over, you will have become famous as the sex fiend of Don Mills."

"Jamal, please!"

One afternoon Romesh came to see him, to pay his sympathies. "Don't worry, Nur," he said. "I've been drumming up support for your case. You can come back, no problem, after the case. That dragonlady Broadbent has shut up her mouth."

Missionary was sitting there waiting to hold court, and he asked Romesh questions about Guyana. He wanted to know how the Indians got along with the blacks, he offered his opinions of the Indian leadership, finishing with: "You know, once I almost advised some young men in Africa to go forth to South America. But something told me no. Now they are here." He sat back with a satisfied sigh. Canada to him was a veritable Amarapur, the eternal city, the land of the west in quest of which his community had embarked some four hundred years ago. This was the final stop. He was very happy.

Missionary's followers started arriving and Romesh got up to leave, throwing a signal to Nurdin, who got up to accompany him. Sushila had come to the centre, he said. To inquire about him, express concern. There was a message from her. Call, she said. Just call. There are other Mondays.

Nurdin was surprised at Romesh's seriousness, his discretion. His regard for Nurdin seemed to have altered quite perceptibly. The incident, it seemed, had in some way touched him too.

17

At the entrance of Sixty-nine Rosecliffe Park, Nanji and Khati got into Jamal's car. Jamal looked visibly impressed with the twosome. "Where to?" asked Khati gaily from the back. Nanji sat forward and turned sideways so he could see Khati and Jamal.

"The Kensington Market," Jamal answered, "where the girl hangs around. The one who's accused Nurdin. I want you as witnesses so there's no funny business." Jamal had started the car but hadn't accelerated, so that there was an interlude with only the steady murmur of the engine. Finally he turned to them: "Well? How do you like it?"

"Oh – the car," said Nanji. "Well, I can tell you, I've never sat in a Mercedes before. Feels good."

"That's how much impressed he is by it. Khati, there's a lot you've got to teach him."

"Oh, don't worry about him. My father's given him a good talking to and he's only sulking." She giggled.

Jamal joined in with his loud cackle. "I can't get over it. Nanji – Missionary's son-in-law!"

Nanji felt hot around the ears. From now on, he thought, if there is one thing I've got to watch carefully, it's to see I don't get engulfed in the Master's shadow. He had told her, warned her of this resolve, in the most solemn terms.

Missionary had summoned him earlier that morning. "What's this I hear that you've been holding my daughter's hand," he said. He looked as pleased as punch.

"You know, Nanji," Jamal was telling him, "this girl's going to have a lot of fun with you."

He didn't tell Jamal that Missionary, for all his jollity, had expected something from him – a commitment, a marriage proposal – and he had obliged. But Missionary was a bargainer of the old school, he had not stopped there. Sherbet was instantly prepared and his former student Zera brought it out, ice-cold and creamy pink with a rich froth of crushed almonds and pistachios, of which all those present partook to seal the engagement. Even that was not enough. Once the engagement was official, the Master, looking around contentedly for a while, then casually turned a little grave and said, "It is our custom not to prolong engagements." The logic had been impeccable, Nanji could not argue. A tentative date for the wedding had been duly set.

It was from this confrontation with Missionary that he and Khati had emerged only an hour ago, and he was a little apprehensive, though not unconscious that he had won a prize.

Jamal parked the car and they emerged from it onto Baldwin Street. They walked up and down, Jamal bobbing, swinging to the reggae music coming clearly from one of the shops. Even on this autumn weekday, the street was quite busy. Smells of bread, cheese, and fruit mingled with those of European sausages and West Indian patties; mangoes were in season in some part of the world and were selling fast here. After they had done a tour of the market, Jamal stopped and said, "I believe she works at the butcher shop up the street."

"So why were we walking around if you already knew that?"

"To get a feel for the place, man. Relax."

Outside the butcher shop a toy monkey on a street vendor's cart beat relentlessly on a drum, drawing a small crowd.

Jamal went inside. He was in pinstripes and looked impressive. In a minute he came out with the girl; she was not very tall, had short hair, dyed blonde, and wore a lot of makeup.

"Miss Baptista," he said to her. "These are the friends of Mr. Lalani whom you've accused. The girl has come here from England – isn't that right? – and they are very concerned. Mr. Lalani, as you are aware, has said it's a mistake. He was only showing concern."

The girl remained silent, leaning against the glass of the shop window. She was chewing gum. Behind her, through the window you could see meat being packaged for the customers by a team of very efficient salesgirls.

"They've come to ask you if you would drop the charges."

She kept chewing, looked insolently past them at a scene on the street: a car parking carelessly, the one behind it honking. The monkey continued its droll rhythm on the drum.

"My friends don't have time, lady," said Jamal impatiently. "Have you considered what you're letting yourself in for in court? As a check on your credibility, your whole personal life is open to me to investigate. And make public."

"Are you threatening me, sir?"

"No, and these are my witnesses. I only want you to understand. It will be unpleasant for both of you; you and the gentleman who stands accused. You both have families."

The girl started walking, nose in the air, hips swinging, not into the shop but down the street. Jamal followed her, raising a hand behind him to stay his friends. They saw him reasoning with the girl, begging, cajoling, whatever.

"There's no stopping Jamal," said Nanji.

"He's something, isn't he?"

Then the girl entered a fish shop, and Jamal followed. Nanji and Khati waited five minutes, ten minutes, on the sidewalk within earshot of the monkey-drummer, then decided to sit at the local bakery and have coffee. They did not speak. There was enough on their minds, real things to discuss, plans to make, but it was much too soon to relinquish the fullness of the moment to mundane questions. Only the present mattered, which they would have stretched forever. Khati faced the window, looking out for Jamal.

Across the street was the greengrocer's, supplied with plenitude and moderately busy. Diagonally opposite was the butcher shop where Maria Baptista worked. Above the greengrocer was an apartment. A woman stood at the window, looking down at them. Seeing her, Khati gave a start, then laughed.

"Strange," she said.

"What?"

"There was a woman at that window opposite, looking at us . . . an Indian woman. Do many Indians live in this area?"

"No."

"Well, she was Indian. On the older side. . . . "

After a while Jamal found them. There was a package in his hand. He looked satisfied but remained standing. "Come on, let's get lunch," he said, and they all walked out.

"Did she agree, then?" Khati asked impatiently.

He nodded. "Everything's fine."

"Well, what happened?" she insisted.

"Let's go to eat," said Jamal.

They sat at a place in Chinatown, all three of them thoughtful, until their lunch specials arrived and were clattered in front of them on the table.

I wonder what really happened, Nanji thought. He decided to break the silence. "So the girl will drop the charges."

"I believe she will."

"Was she just being kind? Is Nurdin innocent?" Khati asked.

Jamal looked not at her but at Nanji. "That could be the finest porgy in town, my friend." He gave a nod at the package in front of him.

The remark took a moment to register.

"What?" Khati exclaimed, loud enough to attract attention.

"You don't have to risk your career!" said Nanji, a little angry. "You simply – "

"No, no, my friends, it's not like that, although I'll admit there was a certain risk involved. That shop she took me to was her brothers' fish shop. They were just waiting for something like this. I pretended not to know Portuguese, of course, but I heard lots of schemes mentioned to rip me off. I told them my friends from England were rich, and would spare no cost for the defence. And I told them I was opening an office in Lisbon. They asked me if I had come to buy fish, and I said I would be glad to buy their porgy."

"An office in Lisbon for what?" Nanji asked.

"Many of them are illegal, and those who are legal have families there. Not to mention friends."

"So we don't know now if Nurdin is innocent or not."

"I think he is. These are fisherfolk. If he was guilty, they would have knifed him – or me when I followed the girl. You should see them with their knives."

That was your quicksilver Jamal, walking on a precipice. What if those Portuguese brothers had trapped him? While he, Nanji, was watching the gum being masticated and wondering what Nurdin saw in the girl, Jamal was probably measuring her up and deciding his next move.

"That's not a bad idea, opening an office in Lisbon," Nanji said. "So what are you now, a roving Statue of Liberty?"

"Yeah, give me your tired and oppressed," Jamal grinned. "I may not open an office in Lisbon, but I have one now in London. And next week I fly to Singapore. There's a minority Muslim community there that wants to emigrate."

18

Across the valley, which lay comatose under the weight of a heavily overcast November evening, the CN Tower peeping over the curtain of shadowy trees blinked its cryptic message at Nurdin Lalani. Behind him in the kitchen his wife's wooden ladle thudded familiarly on her Zanzibari saucepan. The children, Fatima and Hanif, would be back soon for dinner.

Missionary had gone, was visiting the smaller centres around Toronto, and at the Lalanis' home the quiet, though still a little unfamiliar after four weeks of tumult, was welcome. During this period the phone had rung constantly, visitors it seemed were hanging at their door frame with petitions and ailments spiritual and material. After the announcement of the engagement, it seemed the whirlwind had suddenly stopped; Missionary cancelled all appointments and went on tour, announcing that he would at the same time be looking for his own place to stay in some small Ontario town not far from the city.

The charge against Nurdin had been dropped, and some couldn't help noticing Missionary, bidding his farewells, basking in this victory, which was not really his but Jamal's. For Nurdin now there was the job to think of, which he would resume soon. He was not going to let a mere embarrassment rob him of the security the job brought him. There was the several weeks' lost pay to make up, Fatima's university fees to save for. The girl had decided that Arts and Science wasn't so bad after all. She now had her eye on medical school. And Hanif had a sister who was already nagging him about his future prospects.

It seemed to Nurdin that, with the dust settled, some kind of commitment had been wrought from him in the proceedings of the past few weeks. Missionary had exorcized the past, yet how firmly he had also entrenched it in their hearts. Before, the past tried to fix you from a distance, and you looked away; but Missionary had brought it across the chasm, vivid, devoid of mystery. Now it was all over you. And with this past before you, all around you, you take on the future more evenly matched.

That afternoon of opportunity, the tryst he had almost agreed to – and the freedom it would have led him to – now seemed remote and unreal, had receded into the distance, into another and unknowable world.

M.G. VASSANJI was born in Kenya and raised in Tanzania. Before coming to Canada in 1978, he attended M.I.T. in Massachusetts, and he was a writer-in-residence at the University of Iowa in their prestigious International Writing Program. He has also published *The Gunny Sack* (1989), which won a Regional Commonwealth Prize; *Uhuru Street* (1992), a collection of linked short stories, and, most recently, the acclaimed novel *The Book of Secrets* (1994).

M.G. Vassanji lives in Toronto. He is at work on his next novel.